BETRAYAL
SECRETS & LIES

BETRAYAL
SECRETS & LIES

Jordon Hadfield

To order additional copies of this book, contact:
Xlibris
UK TFN: 0800 0148620 (Toll Free inside the UK)
UK Local: 02036 956328 (+44 20 3695 6328 from outside the UK)
www.Xlibrispublishing.co.uk
Orders@Xlibrispublishing.co.uk
818900

"Hello … it's me … I know what you did …"

5 months before…

Kate

Mid-January, a dark and cold morning. The alarm went off at half past six. Yeah, you guessed it: the school run. It wasn't easy having three boys, aged five, seven, and nine. I mean, I'm not saying your life isn't hard, and it was what we signed up to, even though it wasn't planned. I hadn't told the boys that.

"If you're not downstairs in two minutes, I will come up there and drag you out of bed!" I yelled from the hallway. "Are you just going to sit there?"

"Piss off, Kate."

That's my husband-to-be for you. When we first met, he was amazing, but the athletically fit guy who knew exactly how to treat a woman completely changed when the kids came. He turned into a middle-aged, lazy, plump man who kept fixated to the television.

1

The kids came running down the stairs, piling into the kitchen to grab their breakfast.

"Lucas! What have I told you about tucking your shirt into your trousers?"

"Blah blah blah," he replied.

Well, he is five years old; he always replies with some consecutive form of three words. Sometimes I wondered what they get taught at school, as there seemed to be no discipline.

"Right, boys, come on into the car," I said, "I'll be back later, love. Got an important coffee date with Emma. Don't forget to call Martin about the wedding. Bye, love you."

I clutched onto my bag, phone, and keys. I didn't even give him chance to reply as I left. Well, who was I kidding—he would have just grunted and slobbed further into his chair.

The school gates. Always busy with stuck-up parents wishing their kids luck at school. For Chrissake, they weren't leaving forever.

"Go on in; see you later."

They slammed the doors as they left. *Thanks, Mum,* I secretly heard them say in their heads. No manners. I blamed their father.

"There you are, bitch," a voice said.

"I'm sorry—" I turned my head, "*Emma!* Don't do that to me. What are you doing here?"

"I went for a run and saw your car in the distance."

(Well that was a lie; she never runs.)

"Jump in. We'll go for coffee."

Belle's coffee shop. The kind of place that reminds you of how old your grandparents' houses were. The walls were covered in pink, flowery wallpaper; the majority looked grey. Maroon-coloured shelves displayed cracked china ornaments and crockery. It looked ever so dingy. Don't even get me started on Belle, the owner; she was a cow. She definitely hated Emma and I, for no reason whatsoever—well that's not exactly true. We all went to the same secondary school, and things weren't great between us. Anyway, we both sat down at our usual table.

"Two coffees please, Belle," I asked.

She rolled her eyes into the back of her head. "No problem. Coming up."

It was always an effort for her. I mean, it was her job for goodness' sake.

"So, let's talk about the *wedding*!" shrieked Emma as I sat shaking my left knee with an unusually tight grip.

"Yes. The wedding … OK, let me see …" I placed my book down onto the table, frantically flicking through to the page I was last on.

I had Post-it notes sticking out everywhere; it was like a shit version of a student's revision book.

"Ah! There it is … bridesmaids—"

"Well, as chief bridesmaid, can I make a request?" Emma interrupted.

"Go ahead; you seem to be organising everything!" I snapped back with a very harsh tone. I covered my face in my hands. "I'm sorry. I've had a very stressful morning."

I had to be apologetic and blame something. The truth was, she had always tried to control me, ever since we hung out together in high school. We'd known each other all of our lives; our parents were best friends. I'd always had flashbacks to the day she "grew up" in high school. Ever since then, she'd tried to run my life.

It was September 1992—my first day at secondary school. Everything just looked so massive, I was only five feet tall, practically the smallest person in the building. Well, that wasn't exactly true. I met Emma in the cafeteria hall—she was definitely smaller than me. Anyway, we got talking while queuing up for food.

"Come and sit with me and the girls," she said.

"Only if you don't mind," I replied, nervously, as she definitely seemed the type to hang around the popular girls of the school—yes,

even on day one. And I was right. They sat on the back benches. (They didn't even sit on chairs at a table; they were "too cool" for that.)

"Who's that?" asked one of the girls, playing with her chewing gum with her fingers.

"It's my friend Kate." Emma said. I was pretty surprised she had introduced me to the gang.

"Oi, Kate. Go over there and pour your drink over that nerd's head," Emma challenged me.

This was it. The very thing I was petrified about. I didn't want to become a bully. On the other hand, I didn't want to chicken out. I nervously stumbled over to the boy who was sat all alone, quietly, eating his lunch. I took a deep breath in and apologised profoundly in my mind as I poured my freezing cold milkshake over his head. I never felt so bad in all my life, but I knew that was just the start of Emma's bossiness in my life.

"Kate?" said Emma. "You OK?"

I jolted out of my daydream.

"I'm good," I replied, unreassuringly. "Right, back to wedding planning. I'm giving you the job of bridesmaid dresses—and don't forget, they need to match the colour scheme of white and gold. Take my credit card. I want the invoice as soon as." To be honest, I just wanted to get the fuck out of there. I had begun to feel nauseous—oh, and for the record, Belle still hadn't served us our coffees.

"I'll see you soon, Em. Thanks for your *wonderful* service Belle; it's always a pleasure."

I left and stuck my middle finger up through the window, aiming it at Belle, the stuck-up bitch.

I really didn't understand what was up with me lately. I'd had nothing but down moments, and not to mention the flashbacks. Maybe it was the stress of planning the wedding—well, that's what I kept telling myself anyway. But it felt like I was pushing my closest friend away too. *She must hate me. I need help.*

Matt

I'd not always been lazy. Since meeting Kate I'd never needed to lift a finger. She practically did everything. Some people might've called me a *chauvinistic pig*, but that's far from what I was. I still did chores around the house—not seven days a week, but I still picked up my arse from the sofa. I suppose I was slowly morphing into my best mate Martin—*M and M*, we liked to call ourselves. I swear we both thought we were still in the school playground thinking we were the top dogs. In reality, we just pissed off our missuses. *I suppose I have to do what she says.* I grabbed my phone off the table and called him. No answer—straight to voicemail. I tried five times.

"Finally! What took you so long?"

"Was having a shit," he replied. "Nah, just kidding, mate; was on phone to Em. She was saying your missus stormed out the coffee shop."

"For fucksake."

"What ya calling me for anyway?"

"She said I had to phone you about the wedding."

"What about it?"

I didn't have a clue. "Don't know, mate. Probably suits—"

"Nah, stag do!" he said.

Can't exactly plan that—got ages yet.

"Too early, right? I'll pop over to yours, and we can talk suits," I mentioned.

"Boring! But all right, see ya in a bit."

I arrived at Martin's place. He was playing on his PlayStation. "I'll make the tea, shall I?"

"Yeah, mate. Thanks."

Still no physical movement. I swear he's lazier than me. You wouldn't think he's a top lawyer.

"Come on, pal. Get in here. We need to sort important shit out," I said, stirring the teas vigorously. With a few grunts he came staggering in with one hand down his boxers and a can't-be-bothered look on his face. For the record, he could have at least put some clothes on. I understood it was his house, but I didn't want to see his package.

"Why does she want this doing now? The wedding is ages away," he groaned.

Now I understood how Em felt on a day-to-day basis. "You know what she's like. The colour scheme is white and gold, so I was thinking of getting black suits with gold ties?"

"Yeah, sounds good to me."

"You'll have to look online and get them; I believe Kate's given Em the credit card to sort out bridesmaid dresses."

"I'll just let Em know and then she can get them when she goes out shopping," He said.

I suppose people will be wondering why we would have Martin and Emma sort stuff out for us. Well, truth is, we trusted them, and we had other things to sort out, like the cake, venue, and decoration. Also, Kate and I sorted out their wedding three years ago, so they owed us one.

"All right, I'll have a look as soon as. I'm off to shower." He got up, finally removed his hand from his pants, and stretched, letting out a rather loud yawn.

I suppose I'll let myself out.

Kate

I sat nervously in the car. I couldn't do it. Thoughts circulated my mind. I felt like I was on a carousel ride going around and round. I dragged myself out of the car and walked inside to the reception desk.

"Hi … I don't suppose … er … I can see someone?" I stuttered; my mouth felt dry every time I said a word.

"Yes, that will be fine. Go and take a seat, and someone will be out to see you once they're free."

I took a seat, I felt like everyone was staring at me. When I say *everyone,* I mean there was just one other person sat cross-legged reading one of those gossip magazines. The waiting room was kitted out with posters on the walls asking questions; *are you anxious? Do you need medication? Are you depressed?* I felt like it was a quiz. I tried not to look at them, it'd only fill up my brain with nonsense. For all I know I'm probably fine. But I have to come and see a councillor.

"Kate?" I looked up and saw a young lady standing there, armed with a clipboard. I nodded and stood to attention, "if you'd like to follow me." I kept saying *'I can do this'* over and over again in my head.

"I'm Joanna," she said, whilst sat poised at her desk, "so, what is it I can help you with?"

I tried to speak; nothing came out. I felt trapped within my own body. She didn't help either, just sat there opposite me, judging me with her evil, deceitful eyes. I knew this was a bad idea.

"It's OK, take your time, there's no rush." She patronised me.

Actually, for your information I have three kids that need me to pick them up from school, but I can't just suddenly get up and leave, "I'm sorry … I … don't know why I came … er … I'm just wasting your time."

"You're not wasting anybody's time. You need to talk. Tell me what's on your mind."

Well, Joanna, where do I start? My life is just one big mess. I have too much going on. I'm overworked. I've got three young boys. My fiancé does fuck all. See, it's easy for me to think it, I just can't say it, "I think … er … I'm just tired."

No, you're not telling her the truth!

"I need to go and pick my kids up from school. I'm sorry for the trouble."

I picked up my bag and got up to leave.

"Oh, you've got kids?" she said, "I've got a child too, Sebastian. He's twelve years old. Almost a teenager, nightmare."

I paused and sat back down, it was as if she switched on a light in my brain, "I've got three boys, they drive me up the wall some days."

"Wow, I don't envy you at all," she said.

Finally, someone who actually understands.

"So, what made you come here?" she asked.

"I've been having flashbacks. I've been storming out on friends, overworked and due to get married." I blurted out. I felt a sense of relief, suddenly everything felt normal, my shoulders lowered back to where they should be, and my head cleared.

"That's a lot to be taking on, how do you feel now that you've told me?"

"I feel like a weight has been lifted," I sighed, "I don't want to be rude, but I really do have to go and pick my kids up."

"That's OK. Maybe we could do this again sometime? Let's say next Friday, five P.M.?"

"Sounds great."

I left immediately.

Emma

It's been five days since Kate walked out of the coffee shop. Oh, and not the mention she gave me her credit card to buy bridesmaids dresses, best man and groom's suits. That woman has officially lost it. She hadn't even phoned, texted or messaged me.

"Em… Kate called earlier whilst you were in the shower," Martin said, strolling through to the kitchen naked.

"Will you put some clothes on!? Did she!?"

"No, I won't, you love it… yeah she said she'll be coming around later," he said, as he grabbed me from behind and started grinding his naked body against me.

"Stop, Kate might walk in."

"So, what! She might like what she sees." I pushed him off me, "go and put some pants on now!"

He held his hands up as he trotted off back upstairs. That was a sign of saying *I want sex now please.* But, not on my watch. We've been married for three years now, it's what us women do; ban sex for a bit to see how frustrated they get. It'd be fun.

To tell you the truth, I haven't looked or ordered anything for their wedding. I stood with her credit card in my hand just staring at it. Many thoughts were rushing through my head; *keep it Em! Spend all the money! You deserve it after what she's done!* I tried to block it, but I couldn't. It was the truth. Kate only wants me when it suits her. Just because they helped us plan our wedding—which by the way was shit—doesn't mean we have to help them, although we did make a deal when we were young. My thoughts paused as the doorbell rang.

"I'll get it!" shouted Martin, as he came bolting down the stairs, "Kate, you made it. She's in there."

"Does he ever wear clothes!?" Kate laughed as she came into the kitchen to me.

"No, he doesn't," I said, blankly, "he never listens. What is it you've come for?"

I pretended to not know. She laughed, "Seriously?"

Oh shit, she knew I was lying.

"Have you bought the dresses?"

"I … er … I … haven't. I … er … lost your card."

My palms started to sweat. I could feel my face turning red every time I opened my mouth. It was lie after lie after lie.

"It's OK, I have another. Use this one." She reached into her bag and passed me another card. *Fuck*! I knew I was playing a dangerous game. But this was going to make it a whole lot easier.

Kate

I turned around after grabbing my mini cup of water from the fountain and took a seat.

"So, how have you been?" asked Joanna. I took a sip of water, "yeah I've been good thanks."

"Good? Why wasn't it amazing? Or fantastic?" Oh, she's good at reading people. She knows exactly what to say, "I tend to not use adjectives," I said.

"That's OK. I want to know more than just the word *good;* everyone says that," I think next week I might bring in a thesaurus, she might be impressed, "have you had anymore flashbacks?"

"No, I haven't. It's been a week since my last one."
Surely, that's a good sign I thought. I wasn't going to ask her that as she would probably ask me to dig up something from my past.

16

"That's good to hear, but don't presume it won't ever happen again, trust me," She said in a rather husk tone.

What did she mean when she said *trust me*? Was there something I'm missing here? I'm still prone to the fact of it happening again, she didn't need to tell me or unless it's happened to her, in her past. Do I ask? *No.* Of course I can't, she's the counsellor not me. On the other hand, was this a prompt? Did she want me to ask? I had to say something, she was looking at me very suspiciously, "did you used to have flashbacks?" I said.

Shit – instant regret. I could sense the devilish look she was giving me. She cleared her throat, "yes I did," She put down her pen and spun her chair directly opposite me, "well, I used to have them quite frequently around ten years ago. I … er … had a miscarriage, not with my current partner, but with my ex-husband-"

"I'm sorry for asking, you didn't have to tell me all of this."

"No, I do. It helps people, like you, to tell all. I have to show the example. Anyway, where was I? Ah yes, ex-husband, he was useless. He didn't support anything; I saw a glimpse of empathy when I had the miscarriage. He went off the rails, so I had no other option but to stay strong, not just for me, but for him as well."

"But, why, he was an arsehole?" I questioned, she's so brave to tell me all this. This just proved my flashbacks are nowhere near as bad.

"That's where I went wrong, I had no other support. I'd try to talk to him about my feelings, but he'd just shut me down by saying *'get over it, I have.'* It was awful. When he er … died … I felt relieved. I didn't feel trapped and I grieved for my lost child properly, but then the flashbacks happened. I saw a counsellor, eventually, and they stopped."

"He died?" I said, shockingly.

"Yes, he had an overdose," she replied, quickly removing the final tear drop from her face, "right I think our time is up for today, I'll contact you with another date and you can share your story."

"Sounds good to me."

"Thanks Kate." She said as she ushered me out the door. I couldn't help but think there seemed to be more about her ex-husband's death, she had totally changed her mannerisms and stopped crying instantly. It didn't seem to add up.

Emma

I sat at the kitchen table staring at both credit cards, with Kate's name embedded into them. It has been a few weeks, and I still haven't bought anything she wanted for the wedding, I've been moping around the house thinking about what to do.

"Babe?" I shouted through to the living room, "is it wrong if I take Kate's money?"

"Well, yeah, it's fraud. But, no one will find out if it's only us two that knows about it," he said, whilst continuing to play on his console.

I went to grab my notepad from the drawer to start writing a plan. I know I had to be discreet with all of this. I got my laptop from my bag and opened it up. I started to transfer the money from one of the credit cards into my own savings account. Ten thousand pound as easy as that. I felt the guilt rush through me as I smirked at the computer screen. I immediately cut the credit card up into small pieces and threw it into the bin. I knew what I had to do to stop the guilt and that was to use the other credit card to buy the dresses and suits.

I took a trip into town, I visited many shops; *River Island, Topshop, Next,* and *H&M,* but I couldn't find anything that would *fit* the colour scheme.

Some days I questioned my job role; I'm an accountant not a wedding planner. There's too much stress involved with all of this it should be her doing it all, not me. Hence why I'm teaching her a lesson, we've been friends for far too long, she'd believe anything I say or do. I'm good at faking financial accounts, technically I do it for a living.

Anyway, back to the job at hand. At last, a proper wedding shop that sold bridesmaid's dresses and suits, for the men. I vigorously swiped through the rails. There. That's the one. A strapless, gold and white dress. It had a few diamantes around the chest area, which just sparkled constantly with or without a light shining on it. I tried it on. It looked lush.

"Can I have three of these dresses, please?" I said, with a rather fake posh voice—I always felt in places like this you should sound stuck up and very posh.

"Sure thing. What sizes are you after?" said the patronising shop assistant.

"Six, ten, and sixteen."

"Certainly. I'll put them behind the till for you." She elegantly trotted away in her six-inch heels that she definitely couldn't walk in properly, stumbling every two steps she takes. Now, onto the suits. I didn't even bother looking, I just picked the first two I saw, they were the right sizes too. Perfect.

"And these two as well please, lovely."

"That'll be four thousand five hundred pounds then please. Cash or card?"

Is she really asking me that question? *I'll be paying cash, darling, as I always carry almost five thousand pound in my pocket.* The little things annoy me.

"Card," I bluntly stated.

"That's all sorted. Thank you. Have a wonderful day."

I got a text from Kate asking to go to her house. I instantly thought, she found out.

I pulled up outside her house. I can do this, I'm a good liar. She wouldn't have found out; she never uses online banking, as she doesn't know how to work a laptop.

"I'm glad you made it," she said, as she welcomed me inside, "did you get them? Show me?" She was getting very excited, I'll keep talking about the wedding, that'll throw the scent off of what I'd done.

I took the dresses and suits out of the bag. She screamed. I screamed.

"They look amazing! Oh my, the suit … he's going to look fit in that!" she wailed.

"Don't you start crying, you'll set me off."

"Thank you, for doing this. I appreciate it."

"Ah, before I forget, here's your credit card, don't want to lose it like I did the other one."

It was a risk saying that, but I had to make a joke out of it. She didn't even blink. It was a success.

"Before you go, will you and Martin join us for a double date night on Valentine's Day?" She asked.

I didn't know how to respond. I know what Martin's like after a few drinks; he'll say anything to anyone. I don't want him to slip up about my plan to rob more money.

"Yeah, we'll join," I replied.

Why did I agree? I need to make sure my twat of a husband doesn't say anything.

Matt

Valentine's Day. I've always hated it. I'm a believer of showing love every single day in a relationship, not just on one day. Nonetheless, Kate loves it. It's the only day I do everything. Yes, you heard correctly – I do everything! I get up at six thirty doing the kids' packed lunch boxes for school. (Normally, I'd be sleep deprived playing my console.) I quietly sneak into the boys' room and wake them up to get ready for school.

"Boys, it's time to get up for school. Don't wake mum up," I whispered.

I wanted to surprise her to breakfast in bed, once I've done the school run. When I say *"breakfast in bed"* I mean going to the nearest McDonald's and delivering it to the bedroom – she loves it.

School run's done and I'm armed with the breakfast. I crept into the kitchen and took off all my clothes and put on the missus' apron. I place the breakfast on the tray and tiptoed to the bedroom.

"Morning, babe," I said, seductively.

Who said romance was dead? She woke up with a beaming smile, "happy Valentine's day."

"I brought you breakfast, your favourite."

"Thanks, babe. I love you."

I placed the breakfast on the bedside cabinet and straddled over her. We kissed and one thing lead to another.

Emma

Here's the day I've been dreading. I've told Martin on numerous occasions to keep his mouth firmly shut this evening. I can't have Kate knowing what we've done. Yes, I said we, we're both in this together. He clearly doesn't give a shit, he keeps saying, *"it's only ten grand, she owes you it."* He's right in one aspect – she does owe us it. But what we've done is fraud and not to mention betraying our best friends. Martin had no fear inside of him, he isn't scared of anything. Kate called;

"Hi Em, only me. Just calling to see if you could do me a massive favour?"

"Yeah sure, what is it?"

"I've had an email from the wedding venue asking for the full payment by midday tomorrow, is there any chance you could sort it for me, you know I'm no good at technology." I felt the blood rush straight to my head, *"no problem, see you later."*

I put the phone down. I'm not sure if I can continue doing this. I have to come clean; I felt like I was going to slip up and tell her everything.

"Who was that?" Martin asked, walking through half dressed.

"It was Kate, asking if I could sort out the venue for the wedding."

"She has a cheek. To be fair she is shit at online payments. Where's my shirt?"

"In your wardrobe."

He wandered back upstairs.

The venue is charging fifteen thousand pounds, I then thought I could take that and put it into my account, but the guilt ran through me.

Emma

The Copper Valley Restaurant. The perfect place for a romantic dinner date. Kate and Matt were already here, sat poised at the table.

"Evening," Matt said, "isn't this lovely?"

Well, I didn't find it *lovely* at all. We sat here, drinking, having a laugh as if everything is normal. What if I said I've stole ten thousand pounds; would they laugh then? Probably not. I have to put it to the back of my mind.

"Oh Emma. I realised I took back the credit card, here take it to pay for the venue." Kate laughed.

"What you like!? Thanks. I'll do it first thing tomorrow morning."

Little does she know that I won't be doing it. I headed to the toilet. My phone rang; *unknown caller.*

"It's me ... have you done it?"

"Yeah I've took ten grand so far. Another fifteen thousand coming tomorrow."

"Perfect. Come to the shop tomorrow and we'll do it together."

"OK."

"Don't forget the rest of the plan ..."

"I won't."

I splashed my face with water and went back to face the rest of the night.

"You took your time babe." Martin said, sarcastically. I was only gone for ten minutes.

"Yeah had a phone call from Mum." I lied.

We continued to eat, laugh and talk. My next step of the plan would be somewhat risky. I had to destroy their relationship, so their wedding doesn't go ahead and the money, well they wouldn't suspect a thing, they would think it's all been spent on the wedding and no refunds could possibly happen. I stretched my legs under the table and purposely touched Matt's foot. His eyes widened and he shuffled his legs under his chair.

"Sorry," I said, with a smirk.

I *accidently* knocked the table, causing Kate's drink to fall.

"Shit!" she screamed.

"Sorry, my fault, I knocked the table. I'll go and get another drink for you," I said, as I got up to go to the bar. I got her another large wine but added something that would make this plan a whole lot easier; *a sleeping tablet.* I placed the glass elegantly down on the table, "there you go."

"Thank you," She said. She took a big gulp. Wouldn't be long until it started to take an effect. We continued to laugh. Kate's eyes started to close; her head was sinking lower.

"Babe?" Matt said, "you OK?"

"I … I … I … don't feel so well …" she was drifting in and out of sleep.

"I'll take you back, come on."

"No, it's fine, I'll do it, you stay and finish your meal," Martin said. He knew the plan. Matt was itching to leave, checking his phone every two minutes.

"Drink?" I asked.

"No. No, I think I should go, need to check to see if she's alright."

"She will be. Don't worry, Martin's with her."

"Seriously, please, let's just go."

"Fine."

We left and got in the same taxi. Matt was pretty drunk; I don't think he'd remember where we end up. We arrived at my house.

"K … Kate?" Matt stuttered, as he stumbled to what he thought was his hallway, when in fact it was mine.

"Come on, she'll be upstairs." I grabbed his hand and led him upstairs into my bedroom. I started to take his clothes off and kissed him.

"What you are doing!?" he blurted out.

"I know you've always wanted this, Matthew. I saw the look you were giving me tonight; Kate won't mind."

I took off his jeans and sunk lower. He started to sigh and placed his hands through my hair. He was enjoying it.

Matt

Friday 15th February

121 days to the wedding

My head was pounding. I know I say this all the time but that *was* the last time I'm drinking. I lifted my head slowly, it felt like I was on the waltzers at a fairground. I laid back down.

"So, you are awake then," Kate said, bursting into the room, "what time do you call this? It's half past two in the bastard afternoon. I've got to go and pick the kids up in a bit and I don't want them to see you like this. Get yourself showered and look a little more… alive." She slammed the door.

Firstly, how the fuck am I at home? Secondly, I'm in bed naked. Oh shit. Flashback. I had sex with Emma. *Fuck!* I screamed. I dived out of bed and ran straight into the shower. I scrubbed the dirt, the shame and the dignity off my cheating body. I screwed my fists up tight and punched the shower wall. I cried. *Why have I done this?*

What has Kate ever done to deserve this? How do I tell her? I have to speak to Emma.

"Emma! Open up! I know you're in there!" I shouted, as I knocked repetitively. Just answer the flippin' door, it's not that hard.

"What do you want!?" she boomed out her bedroom window.

"I need to talk about what happened last night!"

"We had sex. What more is there to say?"

"Keep it down. Let me in, please."

She closed the window. I paced up and down the driveway. Precisely two minutes later she opened the door.

"Does Martin know?" I asked, with a rather harsh tone. "It was a *big* mistake. You can't tell Kate."

"Calm down. The answer is yes; Martin does know and for the record it's not me that should be telling Kate. You did the deed."

"Fuck off. You initiated it."

"My word against yours. If that's all, you may now leave." *Why is she being like this?* She took advantage, I was drunk.

"Goodbye Matthew." She smirked.

"It's Matt!"

"Whatever."

Belle

Belle. The coffee shop owner. She barely cracks a smile for anyone and yet she is still in business. Her shop stood in the middle of a busy street, serving over fifty customers *(at least)* a day. Her clientele are usually businessmen/women, who stop by on the way to work, for a coffee, or for lunch. She inherited the shop from her parents, who sadly died in a car crash last year – that's why she's not her full self. Nevertheless, she must keep the business afloat, which is proving to be popular. However, most of the press she receives is very negative;

'Avoid, avoid, avoid. Coffee was served cold!' – Anonymous

'Awful service!' – Jon

'Stale bread, cold tea. No sweeteners
available. Avoid at all cost' – Pauline

But it still doesn't affect the business at all. People still pay good money for a *(cold)* coffee. When she closes the shop, she usually spends her time sat at a table, with a large glass of wine, scrolling through the comments. She would cry, smile, or even laugh.

Emma burst through the door. Luckily it wasn't very busy this afternoon, otherwise she'd attract much more attention.

"You got a minute?" she gasped.

"Yeah, take a seat, over here."

"I know you told me to never come to the shop when you're open to talk about this but; it happened."

"What did?"

"I slept with Matt."

Belle wasn't shocked at all. In fact, she came up with the plan. Belle had a lot of history with both Emma and Kate. All three of them went to the same secondary school together. Belle was their victim as they became *bitchier* during year nine. They would steal her dinner money off of her, trip her up on purpose, make her sit on the floor on the school bus and worse of all they embarrassed her in P.E. whilst she was getting dressed. So, it's only right for Belle to get her own back. Even now, she's not particularly keen on Emma, but she knows how much she wants Kate's wedding to be shit compared to her own. The truth is, none of them want or ever have been friends. They're all out to destroy each other's lives.

"Good," Belle said, bluntly.

"Why do you hate me so much?"

"You treated me like shit," She replied with no emotion, "And that bitch Kate. You both deserve to rot in hell, but first I just want payback. You continue to listen and do everything I tell you and I'll call it quits between us two."

"Deal," Emma said through gritted teeth, "what now?"

"I want you to keep taking the money from her and plant this in her house," Belle gave her a box containing a mini CCTV camera, "whatever you do, don't get caught."

"This is risky, Belle. If she finds it, it's game over."

"Well, make sure she doesn't. Bye."

She walked away to serve her customers. Emma threw the box into her bag, "oh and by the way, I took another fifteen thousand pounds. You're welcome."

She stormed out.

Kate

I t's only nine-thirty in the morning and I'm already stressed. I got up at six o'clock and made the kids' packed lunches *(stressful)*, got them up and dressed *(stressful)* and did the school run *(stressful.)* Before I even got out the car, I had a phone call—you guessed it—it was the school; *"Lucas has been sick, it'd be best if you came and picked him up as soon as possible."* That's not the phone call I wanted, so I picked him up *(stressful)* and now he's laid on the sofa watching CBeebies on repeat. I have my next appointment with Joanna in an hour but have no one to look after Lucas *(stressful.)* I can't rely on Matt, he's in bed after a long night shift—on his Xbox—I swear sometimes I think I'm marrying a teenager. It's Ten o'clock, it looked like Lucas was coming with me.

"Mummy, where are we?" Lucas mumbled.

"I have a very important meeting, so I need you to be a good boy, is that OK?" He nodded. "And if you behave, I'll buy you some sweets for you to eat when you're better." His face suddenly lit up, in which I questioned; *is he actually ill?* I mean, of course, he was otherwise the teacher wouldn't have called me.

"Right come on you, let's go in."

Everyone stared at me the second I walked through the door. All their faces in confusion as to why I have brought a small child along to one of my counselling sessions. *(I'm such a bad mum or is Matt a bad dad?)* I continued to pass through and reached Joanna's door.

"Come in," she chirped, as I rushed through in sheer panic. "Oh, you have a companion…"

"I'm so sorry, this is Lucas, my youngest, school called to say he was ill, and I had no one to look after him. Stressful." I raced in one whole breath.

"You seem very tense."

"Well, wouldn't you?" I snapped. "Lucas, please sit still. Stop touching."

"He's alright." She smiled.

Everything in this office looked very expensive and if he breaks something, I just wouldn't be able to afford it. But if she says *"he's alright"* then I'm not paying for any damages.

"In our last meeting I recall myself talking about my issues in the past and this session I want to know more about you. For instance, why are you here? What's causing your *flashbacks*?" she asked.

"I've only had the one major flashback. It seemed to always be about secondary school, which was many years ago. It probably doesn't help that I'm still friends with Emma, who I met in school. She used to try and rule my life, bossing me around, do this, do that. Recently she's been trying to do it again and to save the hassle I let it happen."

"I think we may have found to issue," she said, whilst scribbling rather quickly in her polka-dot book, "maybe it's best you both part ways. It doesn't sound like you are *friends* to me. Is there something else that's stopping you both from not being *friends*?"

"Well, we've always had a deal with one another; *we'd help plan each other's weddings when and if it happens.* She had hers a few years back and mines coming up in June. But the thing is we don't talk every day, we don't meet up every day, a lot of the friendship is toxic. Maybe I'm the problem. I just don't know."

"You should never just blame yourself in situations like this. It's never one sided and if anything, she has had a massive psychological influence in your life, since being very young, and seems to me it's something you just can't let go of."

She was really good. Finally, someone understood what I'm going through, but I can't just betray Emma and our trust with one another, especially with the wedding coming up, that's the last thing I wanted.

"And then there's Belle…" I gritted through my teeth, with a huge amount of disgust covering the circumference of my face.

"She was and has always been a part of this." I continued. You know, I could get to use to this, I felt a wave had blown over me and for some reason my mouth continued to voice many issues.

"Who is this Belle?" Joanna questioned, with her pen poised over her notebook again. Before I began to explain I heard a smash and looked over and saw Lucas, red-faced, standing over a flower vase in shattered pieces.

"I am so sorry." I said, whilst dragging him over to my seat and sat him down on my lap. He didn't know whether to laugh or cry, as I'm sure you know many five-year-old's laughs at anything they do no matter what the consequences are.

"Don't worry about it, I didn't like the vase anyway. If anything, you've done me a favour." Joanna laughed. I breathed with a deep sigh of relief. He was one lucky boy. The smash of the vase kept replaying in my head…

Back at secondary school. We were in year ten, the year before our exams. We were in MR Potts pottery lesson – ironic – and yes, our school did various random lessons, pottery being one of them. Em and I sat next to one another using the pottery wheels to create our vases we designed. Sat opposite us was Belle, she was the quiet one of the class which was a great target for Emma. Belle had almost finished painting her masterpiece, as she stayed after school yesterday creating it, and judging by the look on her face we couldn't tell if she liked it or hated it. Emma gave me a nudge, "go on, smash it."

"I can't do that." I said.

"Oh, come on Kate, you've done far worse to her over the years." Em whispered.

It was true. I only did the things I did because Emma and the gang had told me too. They were bad influences. But none-the-less duty called. I went over, "that's a nice vase" I said, sarcastically. I picked it up and 'accidently' dropped it on the floor.

"Oops." I laughed.

"…I think that just topped it off. I didn't want to be that person. I felt sick that I created misery of a person each day during their entire school life."

"Wow. Now I understand. What you did was definitely wrong on so many levels, but what about now? Have you seen each other since? Did you apologise?" Joanna questioned, whilst she swept up the shattered vase pieces.

"Yes, I did. I apologised at prom. Probably not the ideal place, but I wanted to make a fresh new start. As far as I was aware, she accepted the apology and I presumed she moved on until recently I went to her coffee shop, on the high street, and she's exactly the same—face like a slapped arse." I said.

It's true. I know she tragically lost her parents but needing a familiar face should surely lighten the mood a little and wanting that someone to speak to.

"Well, in your head it seemed things had cleared up, but in actual fact she's probably still grieving her secondary school years,' she said, 'and let me tell you grieving is not an easy process in which I can relate to."

"Why?"

"We haven't got time; your session is over."

I then remember her talking about the miscarriage she had, maybe that was the reason or something else?

"Come on Lucas, time to go. Thanks Joanna this session really helped."

"It's my job and please call me Jo."

"Thanks… Jo."

We got back into the car and grabbed my phone. I called Matt;

"Hey babe, it's me. I'm just picking the kids up from school. I left tea wrapped in foil in the fridge, could you take it out and pop it into the oven, please?"

"Yeah babe."

"Thanks, see you in a bit, love you."

"Love you."

We returned home and to my surprise the house was pristine to the point where I didn't even recognise it. the smell of the food in the oven drowned out the air fresheners. There was no sign of the kids' toys on the floor and everything just looked so clean.

"Right, kids go wash your hands, tea will be served in a bit," I said, they bolted upstairs to the bathroom, "someone's been busy."

"You see I'm not a waste of a man." He growled, as he lifted me slightly off the ground, spun me, then gave me a sloppy snog. He's certainly still got it.

"Have you heard anything from Em or Martin about the wedding plans?" I asked.

"Nothing. They've been very quiet," he replied, whilst taking the pasta bake out of the oven.

"They've probably got a surprise up their sleeves knowing them," I tried to convince myself, "that apron looks fit on you." *(I had to change the subject.)* It's a shame the kids are in otherwise it'd be on the floor and that kitchen table would have taken a good beating.

"Maybe I'll wear it later on when we go to bed and slowly remove it revealing nothing underneath," he seduced me.

Something's definitely changed inside of him as this behaviour doesn't normally happen. I shouldn't start over thinking it, I quite like it when he's in this sort of mood.

Emma

Since the conversation I had with Belle, I haven't left the house. I've practically locked myself in. I already felt guilty about stealing the money and now she wanted me to plant a CCTV camera in Kate's house. That's just weird. I've received endless messages from Belle saying;

'Is it done yet?'

'Hello? You there?'

'Why are you ignoring me?'

'I need you to plant the camera ASAP!'

I haven't responded to any. My heart sank as my phone rang; it was Kate. I didn't answer. I wait for the dreaded notification; *you have 1 voicemail, click now to listen.* I hover my finger over the button, I couldn't bring myself to press it, I was scared in case she found out about everything, but I had to listen;

44

"Hi Em, it's me. The wedding is coming up quicker than I'd like, over a hundred days now, I just need the invoices sent through today to show evidence everything is booked, and I'll stop myself from panicking and going crazy if things are last minute."

Shit. Shit. Shit. This couldn't be happening. I mean I knew it would be, but I'm so not prepared for this. She wanted them *today*. I can't keep making excuses, she knows I *'have sorted things'* as I told her I had. I can feel my face boiling up, I'm sure it'd look as red as if I've been sat outside in the sun all day. I'd have to tell her the truth, but I wouldn't be able to. My head told me one thing and my heart told me another. A text:

'Have you planted the camera yet?' – Belle

Fuck off Belle, can't you see I have a massive problem I need to sort out first? I grabbed my laptop and search *fake invoice templates* on Google. Lots of results appeared, I selected one and began to fill in the blanks. It's a huge operation as I have to copy and paste the logos of companies I used, to make them look legit; Kate won't be able to tell the difference she'll just be pleased it's all *sorted*. But then I think; *what if she phones up the companies to triple check?* No, she won't, I convinced myself. I'll *accidently* forget to write the phone numbers down on the invoices, that'd solve the issue. (She won't be able to tell the difference.) It's easier when there's a template that's already made up. I printed them and make my way to Kate's.

I arrived with the *(fake)* invoices and CCTV camera in my bag ready to be planted.

"Kate!" I shouted, as I walked through the house, "I have your invoices you requested. Kate?"

She wasn't there. The door was unlocked, but no one seemed to be in. I tip-toed up the stairs and tried to be as quiet as I can. Her bedroom door was closed, I presumed she was in there and wanted to scare her, so I burst through the door. I screamed. Kate screamed. Matt screamed. I walked in on them having sex.

"Cover yourselves up!" I demanded, whilst I covered my eyes, avoiding seeing them naked.

"Emma, what are you doing here?" she panted.

"I came to drop the invoices off that you asked for. The door was open, so I let myself in."

I mean I wasn't that shocked as I've seen all of Matt's body parts before, I could see the panic on his face whilst struggling to keep hold of the tiny pillow to cover his modesty. He was giving the look of *don't you dare say what happened between us.* I wasn't going to. She will find out eventually.

"Can you go back downstairs please? I'll be down in a minute." She asked.

I left and waited downstairs. As I waited, I remembered about the camera. I found a discreet place; the plant pot that stood in the corner of the living room. I linked up the camera to my phone to test to see if everything was in view—and it was. It seemed to be a good quality camera. I gave Belle a text saying; *"done."* That should keep her off my back—for now at least. They both walked into the living room, embarrassed.

"Sorry about that," I said, "don't worry about it, I've seen it all before." I winked at Matt. Kate didn't notice.

"What?" she questioned.

"You know, body parts and all," I laughed, "well, here are the invoices."

She took them off me and walked through to the kitchen to grab her folder to place them in. She didn't even look at them. I went to follow, but Matt grabbed my arm, "what are you thinking? Saying that!" he whispered, holding a very firm grip on my arm.

"You see, it's easy to wind you up. Let go of my arm you're hurting me."

"You'll regret this."

He let go of me.

"Is that a threat? Just remember who you're dealing with. You're a nobody—"

"Em, come here," Kate interrupted.

I squinted my eyes and sassed my way into the kitchen.

"The wedding is pretty much all planned, there's just one more thing," She said.

"What is it?"

"My dress. I phoned up the shop and I booked an appointment for us on Monday. Please say you can make it?"

She gave me the *puppy dog eyes.* I couldn't let her down and besides the dress is the most important thing and I'm pretty sure I could be nice for just one day.

"Yes of course." I smiled.

Kate

The day I have always dreamed of had arrived! I have cleared my entire schedule to go and choose my *perfect* wedding dress and I wanted no distractions.

"Babe, today is a very important day, I need you to do everything, if that's OK?"

"I haven't really got a choice in the matter, but yes madam you can count on me," He said, as he wrapped his arms around me, from behind, and kissed my neck.

"I said no distractions! Now go, the kids need to get to school," I demanded.

"And I already said you can count on me!"

It's true, I can. He really had started to pull his weight these past few weeks, I wondered what's got into him. I'm not complaining, but he only does this sort of thing when he's done something he shouldn't have. But one way or another I will find out and for now I will keep going along with it.

"Emma's at the door," Matt charged in.

"Amazing. I'll see you tonight."

We arrived at the shop and within seconds I instantly caught the butterflies in my stomach. All the dresses on display looked so lovely and to think one of them was going to be mine that I wear on my (very) special day is amazing.

"Hello ladies. I'm Carol and I'll be helping you pick your wedding dress today," she kindly welcomed us, "so, which lucky lady is getting married?"

"I am," I said.

"What type of dress are you looking for?"

"Such a tough decision, I prefer white, sparkly, long, and nicely fitted against my body shape." (Honestly, I'm not that picky.)

"Lovely, take a look on the rails and give me a shout when you're ready to try one on."

Emma and I grabbed a half-filled glass of (cheap) champagne as I began to browse through the endless array of wedding dresses. There are so many dresses to choose from, I just didn't know where to start. I saw a budget rail and that's definitely not what I want. At least that's a quarter of the shop I won't be looking at.

"Have you found one?" Emma asked, impatiently.

"No, I haven't, what's the rush?" I reply, whilst I continued the search.

"No reason."

"Well, maybe if you get off your phone and actually help then we'll be done quicker."

She (finally) put her phone down and started to help. But it was too late. I found it. The perfect dress was staring right in front of me. It was long, white and sparkly, with a huge trail. The diamantes on the chest area seemed to glisten in the light.

"Carol. Sorry love, I would like to try this one on?" I beamed with delight.

"Lovely, follow me."

I squeezed all my assets into this very tight-fitted dress (just what I wanted) and it looked perfect. I wept tears of happiness, as I stared into the mirror, taking it all in.

"Em, what do you think?" I sniffled.

"Yeah, it looks lush," she replied, "I'm really sorry, I have to go."

"You can't just walk out, it's a special moment," I shrieked.

"I'll pop by later."

And that was that. She left. Generally, it felt as if I was jilted at the altar. It was strange for her to just leave like that. I instantly thought she was hiding something. First my fiancé and now my best friend. I think no more of it and get back in the moment of staring at myself in this (perfect) dress.

"I'll take it."

Emma

I had to leave, sharpest. Belle text; *meet me at the coffee shop now. Urgent.* And believe me, when Belle says it's *urgent,* she means it's *urgent.* I was rushing through the crowds of people on the high street, pushing by people who stopped in the middle of the path to have a conversation. (Rude.) Forever, tutting my way through, passing people who stood to take a selfie. (Rude.) I wish people had the decency to care for those who simply just want to walk (quickly) down the street. It's simple, pull to the side and you'll be out of the way.

Nevertheless, I arrived at the coffee shop.

"You're late," she shrieked.

"I'm sorry, I was wedding dress shopping with-"

"Shut up, I don't want to hear it," she rudely interrupted, "follow me, down here."

I followed her into, what looked like, a basement. It was dark, dingy, and the odour of damp fulfilled the small room. She flicked on a switch the place lit up with office beam lights, it looked very much like an interrogation room. There were tables along the wall with computer screens, blacked out, on them. It all seemed very strange.

"Well, what do you think?" she asked.

"It's a basement…" I said, with a confused look on my face, "I don't understand."

"It's my secret room. These computers link up to the CCTV camera you planted. I can sit in comfort and spy on Kate," she blurted out. This room definitely didn't look comfy, but then again, she seemed to be turning into a psychopath, so I'm sure she loved the dark and dampness.

"Yeah… it looks good if you like this sort of thing." I mimicked. If looks could kill, she would definitely of committed her first murder.

"I think it's time we move up a level to get closer in taking down Kate…" she said.

I gulped.

"From this day forward we closely monitor all of Kate's actions. We need to know her every movement and everyone she comes into contact with."

"But what's this going to achieve?"

"Well, we need to know exactly where and what she is doing, so we can continue to sabotage her wedding."

It was all making sense. I knew she wants revenge and the deal was to sabotage her wedding not her entire life. I knew I shouldn't have got involved in all of this. I could just about cope with lying and stealing money, but certainly not spying on her in the privacy of her own home.

"Oh, and Emma a word of warning; don't think about stepping a foot out of place. I will find out and come for you. Got it?"

"Yes." I stuttered.

I felt faint. This definitely wasn't the end; it was just the beginning.

Emma

Friday 15th March

93 days to the wedding

Two weeks into the whole *spying* plan, that Belle practically threatened upon me, I've been stressed to the max. The truth is I've not been feeling too good lately. It's been off and on for quite a while. Some mornings I dread to get out of bed (not because of Belle) because I get really bad stomach pains, it felt like a dagger going through it. It's excruciating. And the minute I do get out of bed I (painfully) run to the toilet and throw up everywhere. But, because of this whole situation with Belle I haven't had time to focus on myself and I realised I missed my period the end of last month. I fear I may be pregnant. I texted Belle;

"I'm sorry Belle, I'm not feeling well. I'm giving today a miss. Sorry. x"

She immediately text back;

"K."

Shit. She's mad. No-one messages back with just a *"K."* That's the symbol of *I fucking hate you.* But, at least today I can focus on myself and find out if this illness is me being "pregnant" or "just ill."

I took a trip to the pharmacy, as I know I'd have no luck in seeing a doctor at a hospital and would have to wait forever. Plus, it's easier to get a test and do it yourself. I picked up a multipack of two. (I never trust just one result.) Not only do I have to bring myself to do the test, but also, I have to tell Martin and Matt. I suddenly froze in the pharmacy.

"Excuse me miss, do you need any help?" the shop assistant said.

"I'm pregnant," I blurted out. Instant regret. I quickly snapped out of it and stared right at the man in uniform, with his name **'MARK'** written in bold on his badge, "I'm sorry Mark." Even saying his name made it sound even more weird. He didn't even know what to say back. He nodded, raised his eyebrows and walked off.

I returned home. Martin came running down the stairs in a towel, soaking wet.

"Where have you been this morning?" he questioned.

"Nowhere," I said, quietly.

"Something's wrong, you're so pale, it looks like you've seen a ghost."

"I'm pregnant." I murmured.

"What?"

"I'm pregnant!"

He paused.

"I think I'm pregnant…" I said.

"It's simple, you are or you're not."

"I've got the test; I can't bring myself to do it."

"You have to, we need to know," he held my hands, "I know it's scary. It's life-changing, not just for you, but for us. Now come on, wipe them tears away and do it, otherwise you'll never know."

It's true. He knew about Matt and I sleeping together and he's still sticking beside me. I needed to do the test.

"I'll be right outside the bathroom door."

I kissed him and went in. I did what I had to do and waited for the results. I couldn't bear to look at it. Martin knocked on the door, "everything alright in there?"

"You can come in babe; we'll look at it together."

He burst in in excitement.

"You ready?" he said.

"Yes."

I took a deep breath in. "It's… positive." I cried.

"I love you," He beamed.

But there was one problem; I needed to tell Matt.

Emma

I was banging on his door for ages. He finally swung it open, "what do you want!?" he boomed. Little did he know I'm (potentially) about to destroy his life forever.

"I need to speak to you," I said, calmly. It's a trick I learnt; *always stay calm when someone has a temper.*

"What is it? I'm not playing any of your stupid games. What happened between us was a mistake and that's all it will ever be," he said, "besides, we've already spoken about this."

He's certainly not wrong.

"I'm…" I stopped.

I can't say it.

"Spit it out…" he urged.

"I'm pregnant."

There. I said it.

"Fuck off."

His mood instantly changed. From anger to shock in a matter of seconds.

"Who's the dad?" he asked.

"It's fifty-fifty."

"Well, how about you get this into your head, I'm not and never will be the dad. Convince yourself it's one hundred percent Martin's baby. Now, piss off and leave me alone, the only time I want to see your face is at the wedding."

"But—"

"Forget it!"

He slammed the door shut.

What have I done? I dragged myself away from his house and started to walk. I'm not entirely sure where I was walking to, but I just kept going. I clenched my fists and stared blankly into the distance as tears rolled down my face. People passed by me would whisper to one another; *"is she alright?"*, *"she looks ill."* I wouldn't even acknowledge them. I turned a corner and sank to my knees. I cried. I screamed. I was broken and no one could fix me.

Kate

Back at Joanna's office for another counselling session. The real reason why I came back this time was to find out more about her. The way she had been acting and the things she had been saying have raised alerts in my head to piece together to find out the truth about her. She's been very mysterious. But whenever I'd raise a question we'd always *"run out of time."* Maybe it's time I counselled her.

"Morning Kate," she said, clutching her cup of coffee in her hands, "do excuse me. I've barely had chance to wake up."

She wasn't wrong. She looked a mess. Her eyes were blood shot and mascara stains on her cheeks. She clearly had a rough night.

"Go anywhere nice?" I asked, politely.

"Just went out for a few drinks."

A few? Doubt it. She definitely walked back through the door five minutes ago. With the state she was in, I'm sure she will tell all, not just about her *night out* but her entire life story.

"I should have cancelled this meeting," she moaned, "I feel sick. I apologise in advance."

I've never seen a counsellor like this. She has a child too. What was she thinking?

"That's OK," I said, through my gritted teeth.

"So, in the follow up to the last session, where are we?"

Why is she asking me? She should know considering she wrote it all in her pad.

"I told you about Belle and you spoke about your own grieving…" I replied.

This was it, I thought, she had to tell me all now.

"Did I?" she asked.

Shit.

"Oh wait, I think I remember. Yes, I did. The truth is…" she continued.

This is the moment I needed.

"I've not been very truthful to you. I like to be honest with all of my clients," she paused to take a sip of coffee, "I do recall telling you that I had a miscarriage and tragically lost my husband, well to tell you the truth a few years back I had completely lost the plot, mentally.

My husband got murdered. And it was all my fault. I had a lawyer involved and thankfully it worked out on my side."

What. The. Fuck. This threw me by surprise. There's definitely lots of gaps with what she was saying, I needed to investigate further.

"Who was your lawyer?" I asked.

"Martin Miller. He was great."

This doesn't add up. Martin is Emma's *lazy* husband. I knew he worked for a law firm, but I'm sure he quit a while back. I needed to contact him and find out everything.

"Oh shit. Sorry Jo, I need to go. Kids are going crazy." I lied. She won't have a clue; she's still pissed from last night. She grunted and belched, as I left.

I rushed into the car and phoned Martin, immediately. No answer. I tried again. No answer. I mean, seriously what is the point of having a phone if you're not going to answer it? It looks like I had to go and pay him a visit.

Kate

What a coincidence, I arrived to find their curtains closed. No wonder he didn't answer his phone, they were still in bed. Besides, this is urgent, I needed to speak to him. I got out the car and rang the doorbell several times. Emma answered.

"Kate? What are you doing here?" she asked, with a puzzled look on her face.

"I'm here to see Martin. I need to talk to him," I said, quickly.

"Come in, I'll put the kettle on."

Inside, Martin was nowhere to be seen. I need Emma out; she didn't need to know about Joanna. Also, she has no idea about me seeing a counsellor.

"He's upstairs in bed. I'll go and tell him you're here." Emma smiled.

I got a text from Joanna, it read:

Ignore what I said earlier, it was the drink talking. Next time I'll be sober and back to my usual self. Take care, see you again. Jo x

She's realised what she said to me was the wrong thing to do, but she can't backtrack now. Since day one, I knew my suspicions were right about her. Although, I didn't expect anything like this to come out of her mouth. Martin came downstairs in nothing but his pants *(as always)* once again.

"Hey Kate. Em said you needed to talk?" He yawned.

He definitely had just woken up.

"Yes. It's about one of your previous clients."

"You know I'm not allowed to talk about anything," he demanded, "it's confidential."

I knew this would happen, "But, you're not a lawyer anymore?"

"I am. Well, I do little bits of it, just not as much as I used too."

"Exactly. No one will find out. Does Joanna Underwood mean anything to you?"

That was it. His face dropped the minute I mentioned her name. Surely, this wasn't going to end well.

"What do you want to know?" he asked.

"Everything."

"You sure about this? There's no turning back."

This must be bad.

"Yes, of course. She's been my counsellor for weeks; I need to know who she is. She practically told me in very few words."

This is hard work.

"Well I suggest you take a seat," he gestured, "you need to be careful; Joanna is unhinged. She's very good at what she does, but she *will* brain wash you. I was roped into helping her fifteen years ago. She had a miscarriage with her 'abusive partner', Damian. Well, that's what she told me. It turned out she damaged him."

I was shocked.

"Really?" I interrupted.

"Yeah, like I said, she's good at what she does. Anyway, fifteen years ago she murdered him. To this day she still classes it as *self-defence*. It wasn't. They had a massive argument and she hit him over the head with an ornament. He was killed in cold blood."

"How is she getting away with this?" I asked.

"She bribed me. She knows a lot of bad people that would 'mess me up,' she says, I had to create a case against Damian and said it was all him being abusive and, sadly, he wasn't there to defend himself. She's a dangerous woman."

I can't believe it. This woman is a counsellor, how on earth is she like this? I noticed Emma was stood in the hallway, trying to hide behind the door.

"I can see you Em," I blurted, "you can't say a word to anyone. Got it?"

She nodded.

"I need to go; this is too much to process."

"Seriously Kate, you can't tell anyone, not even Joanna," Matt said, concerningly.

Emma

Thursday 28th March

80 days to the wedding

I've had too many sleepless nights. First Belle. And now knowing about Kate seeing a counsellor, who in fact is a murderer that my husband helped cover up. It's all too much to process. When (or if) Kate finds out about me stealing money from her, she'll be pissed off and blame me – in which she'll have the right to, but she'll ignore how damaged I am. I received a text from Belle: *Basement now!*

I arrived at the coffee shop to find out what Belle wants this time. She's been very quiet lately since I bailed on her as I needed some time to myself.

"You texted," I said, as I walked down the stairs leading to the basement.

"Oh, so you are alive!" she said, harshly, "I thought you were going to bail on me again. Yanno, like last time?"

Fuck sake. She's pissed off.

"I wasn't feeling too well. Lady problems."

She stared right through me as if to say, *"so what, we all have issues."*

"Anyway, who cares, back to business. The wedding is almost here. We need to sabotage further," Belle continued.

When she says *we* she means *you,* she does fuck all. She'll dictate from her damp basement and happily watch you panic, whilst stealing money for her.

"I have decided I will step up and introduce myself," She said.

"Kate knows who you are."

"Yes, she may know me as Belle, but she doesn't know—"

She grabbed a short blonde wig from a bag and threw it on her head.

"—Lucy."

"But it looks exactly like you, in a wig?"

"I'll wear make-up and dress completely different; I've thought all of this through."

She really had lost the plot. Whatever crazy idea she had come up with would never work. Kate would recognise her within seconds. But, saying that she had no idea about the money being stolen and, of course, there'd be no actual wedding.

"From now on, whenever we're out in public you address me as 'Lucy' and when we are in the basement you can call me Belle," She told me.

"This is crazy!" I stated.

"Do not call me crazy!" she snapped back. It seemed she hated that word. Maybe I'll think it rather than saying it out loud. The last thing I wanted was to get on the wrong side of Belle (Lucy or whoever she is.)

"Right, the plan is," Belle proceeded, "you need to introduce me to Kate, as your *best friend* and secure an invite to the wedding. That way we can find out more information and steal even more money." This was the worst idea ever.

"Take a look here," She said, as she pointed to the computer screen. It showed Kate in her house, filing papers and Matt lounging in his CK boxers playing his games console. No sign of the kids, but then again it is mid-afternoon, they'd still be at school.

"We need our hands on those papers," Belle said, with a mysterious look on her face.

"Got it," I replied, "get that wig on."

We had no option but to go to Kate's house now, as the last thing I wanted was to hurt the kids and get them involved in all of this. I still do feel bad, but I understand why Belle was doing it. I knocked on the door. I can't slip up now. I must remember Belle is now Lucy.

"Hey Em," Kate answered, "what are you doing here?"

"We've come to talk wedding plans!" I said, excitedly, which I hoped didn't sound too fake.

"Who's we?" she asked.

"Oh, sorry, allow me to introduce Lucy."

"And who is Lucy?"

"She was my best friend back on my old housing estate. She's recently moved next door to us," I lied.

She seemed to be really taking this literally. This was easy. Well done Belle, I mean, Lucy.

"Well don't just stand there, come on in and you can tell me all about how you both met." Kate cheered.

Oh shit, maybe it's not that easy. Maybe she knew. Maybe she knew the whole truth about the money, the wedding, everything. Belle (Lucy) noticed my panicked face and nudged me as we walked in.

"Remember, act normal!" she whispered, sharply, as we walked through seeing Matt in his CK's—*again.*

"Move it, we're talking weddings." Kate told Matt. He huffed as he rearranged his tightly fitted underwear and stormed upstairs. He didn't even acknowledge me. I couldn't help but stare at his package, what Kate didn't realise was that I'd seen it all and he may have got me pregnant.

"Sorry about him," Kate said, "so, tell me all."

The three dreaded words – *tell me all* – are the worst. We haven't had time to rehearse this, I've no idea what to say. Whatever came out was a lie and what if I slip up? I must speak, I can feel Belle's (Lucy's) dagger eyes staring at me.

"So, yeah, Lucy and I were friends on the council estate we lived in when I were seven, I think it was," I lied.

"Yeah it was, hun. It was the best few years of my life. Moving to a new estate is scary, but then I met you and you just helped me settle down. We had such a laugh." Belle (Lucy) said, with an awful imitation of an Essex accent.

"Aw," Kate said, bluntly, "Em, can I have a word in private please?"

"Sure."

We headed into the kitchen, leaving Belle (Lucy) sat twiddling her thumbs.

"Is she legit?" Kate asked.

"Yes. It's very sudden. She turned up today, I was gobsmacked," I lied, again, "I do have something else I'd like to ask."

"Go ahead."

"Maybe she could come to the wedding?"

"Really? I don't even know her."

"But you know me. Honestly, she's harmless. Pretty please?" I begged.

We just needed Kate to accept and that way Belle (Lucy) could continue with her plan.

"Hmm. OK. Yes. She can come to the wedding." She said, with very little excitement.

"Also, she may need to help me with the hen party."

"That's fine, I don't want to stress over the hen party, that's the only time I will just turn up and enjoy myself without the stress."

"Deal."

We headed back into the living room. I gave Belle (Lucy) the nod of acceptance.

"Come on then, we best be off, got a hen party to plan." I said to Belle (Lucy.)

Matt

Today is the day I dreaded. It's my birthday. I hate birthdays, I see it as a countdown to my death. I know it sounds dark, but it's how I think of it. Kate is the complete opposite. She *loves* a celebration. Any excuse to have a party, she'll do it.

There's nothing better than to get up at six in the morning and run a nice hot bath, it feels more reasonable to do it on your birthday morning. Especially, when the kids are asleep and still in bed. I tiptoed around to try not to wake anyone up. I grabbed a towel from the shelf in my wardrobe and carefully crept into the bathroom. I quietly closed the door and slid the lock in place, as there's nothing worse than someone barging in to have a piss or a shit. I got undressed and climbed into the bath. The steam rising and the hot water covered my body, whilst I sank into the tub. I laid backwards, closed my eyes and took a huge breath in and went under the water.

Whilst under the water, I kept my eyes closed and I pictured my wedding day. It's what I thought of to relax. It's going to be the most perfect day ever. To me that's the day I'm always going to look forward to and celebrate hard.

All of a sudden, I heard a loud bang. I opened my eyes and realised I'm still under the water, I lifted up and started coughing after inhaling quite a bit of water. I heard Kate's voice, "Matt, you in there? You've locked the door?"

"Yes, hold on, I'm in the bath. Just getting out."
I grabbed my towel and stepped out the bath and wrapped myself up. I opened the door.

"Happy birthday babe!" she squealed, as she hugged me tightly. I couldn't have five minutes peace. I can already see that today was going to be a long ass day!

Kate

I love birthdays! I mean in all honestly, I just love a party. I always make sure I'm the first one to get up and give Matt a huge hug and wish him a *happy birthday* before the kids. I've done that so now I continued with today's celebrations.

First, I headed into the kitchen and cooked everyone breakfast; Matt's was a mega breakfast, of course.

"Kids, breakfast's ready." I shouted, at the bottom of the stairs. They came running downstairs faster than any other morning.

"Where's daddy?" Will asked.

"He's just getting ready," I said, "he'll be down soon."

"OK."

"I'm here," Matt said, as he walked through into the kitchen. All three of them ran up to him and screamed *happy birthday*. I had to take a picture. It was really cute.

"What's the plan for today?" he asked.

"We're having a party!" I exclaimed. "Once the kids are back from school, we'll invite a few friends and have a little party."

The kids were very excited and didn't want to go to school. But they have to and that way we can decorate in peace and quiet.

"Come on you three, let's go," I said.

After dropping the kids off at school, I parked up in Asda's car park. I have to grab a few bits and pieces for later on. Whilst shopping around I texted Em saying:

Party at mine tonight for Matt's birthday, feel free to pop along. P.S. bring Lucy too. x

I had to invite Lucy too, it'd be nice to get to know her a little bit more, but if I'm brutally honest, I think she's hiding a lot. My instincts tend to be correct; they were with Joanna.

I left Asda with three shopping bags full of party nibbles and drinks. I received a reply from Em:

Sounds great. We'll be there. x

And so, another investigation begins.

Emma

Two hours until the party and I haven't even started to get ready. I've been worried all day, mixing alcohol with secrets and lies, wrapping around you, do not go together well. I'm frightened I'll say something I shouldn't, or worse Belle's wig falling off or she gets too drunk and tells all. It's risky. I've seen it happen in many films; everyone gets their comeuppance eventually. It's like a ticking time bomb. Although, that was the risk I was willing to take at the start of all of this. I have the days I doubt it and today was one of those days. I received a text from Belle:

Meet me, you know where, in 5 mins.

What she meant by that is; *meet in the basement.* I don't know why she won't just text it. She probably thinks the police or private investigators are searching for clues, so she'll communicate in coded words, which definitely sounded more suspicious.

I arrived at the basement. All the lights are out. How strange? She said *five minutes*, I definitely made it in three minutes. (I know what she's like for lateness.) I slowly walked down the mis-shaped wooden stairs. I stroked the wall to feel for the light switch, I found it and switched it on. I screamed!

"Belle! What the fuck have you done!?" I shouted.

Belle was laid on the floor in a pool of blood, with a *knife* sticking out of her chest. She opened her eyes, "APRIL FOOLS!" she laughed.

"That wasn't funny at all!" I shrieked. "I know you hate the word, but that was crazy, with a capital C!"

She continued to laugh.

"You could have fucking warned me."

"But then it wouldn't have been a hilarious prank."

"It wasn't *hilarious* in the first place! Now, hurry up and clean yourself up, we need to go to the party before Kate panics and calls me."

After cleaning up and getting Belle into Lucy's attire, we arrived at Kate's house, ready for Matt's birthday party.

"No funny business!" I exclaimed to Belle, before walking inside.

"Thanks for coming, ladies," Kate said. "I'll take Matt's presents and pop them with the rest of them."

I gave her a wrapped-up present, that clearly looked like a child had done it. I went over to Matt.

"Happy birthday, sexy," I said, seductively.

"Don't start, Em. Does Kate know you're pregnant?" he barked.

"No. And you can't say anything about it."

"You'll have to tell her sooner or later, before you start showing." He walked off. He wouldn't tell her anyway, as he's the one that's most likely to have knocked me up. Let's face it, he wouldn't want Kate to know that secret.

"Presents!" Kate squealed, "come on everyone, gather round, it's time for Matt to open his presents."

You could see the embarrassment on his face. It felt like a children's party. But Kate had always been like this. We all sat in a circle, as if we were about to play pass the parcel, watching Matt open his presents. He got socks, pants (standard), a couple of CDs and a very sexy red latex brief – *from me.* Thankfully Kate found it hilarious.

"Maybe you should try that on later, babe." She laughed.

He scowled at me. I smirked. I looked away and noticed Belle (Lucy) had vanished.

"Just popping to the toilet," I lied.

I walked off to find her. I saw her in Kate's bedroom carrying a load of paper.

"What are you doing!?" I snapped.

"Finding clues," She said.

"Clues for what?"

"You know," she said, "letters, bank statements, invoices and any evidence that can be traced back to us! I had to grab that folder." She had a point.

"Hurry up, before she notices."

I returned back to the circle; Kate didn't even bat an eyelid. Shortly, after Matt had finished opening his presents, Belle (Lucy) came back with her bag full of papers.

"I'm going. I'll contact you with our next steps once I've scanned through all of this, may take me a while," She mumbled.

"OK."

She left. Kate turned the lights off and came through with the cake. We all sang *happy birthday,* mostly out of tune.

"Make a wish." She told Matt.

He shut his eyes and blew the candles out. Why am I turned on by him? We only had sex once. And besides, I'm married to Martin, who hadn't even turned up to his best friend's party. I mean I don't blame him considering he's hiding secrets from him; you know what men are like with keeping them a secret. It's all getting too much for me, the party, the sexual tension, the secrets, the lies, everything! I left.

Kate

I t's confrontation day. Ever since knowing about Joanna's past I had been wanting to speak to her. The main question was; *is she actually a counsellor?* And that question should be answered in the first fifteen seconds of me entering the room as she wouldn't even remember what happened during our previous session. She was still wasted from the night before, potentially the same morning in fact.

Now that Matt is doing the school run, I didn't need to rush around, I took my time and prepared myself. I grabbed my belongings and headed for a counselling session that Joanna would never forget.

I took a deep breath in and flung open her office door. She jumped.

"Kate?" she stuttered, "What are you doing here?"

"Did your receptionist not tell you?" I smirked.

"Tell me what?"

She was very confused. (Great start.)

"I booked in for another session. I took your first slot of the day." I smiled.

She remained confused, "they failed to tell me. I'll be with you in just a second. Grab a seat."

She started to type viciously on her keyboard, she was clearly typing an email to her receptionist about this.

"Maybe you should get a new receptionist," I joked.

She didn't find it amusing, not even a little smirk. She was acting very shifty. She's probably embarrassed with what happened in our last meeting.

"I see you're sober today." I laughed.

"Yes. I learnt my lesson," She said, bluntly.

I tried to keep making small talk, but I didn't want to make it too weird. I needed to get to the point, but we hadn't started the session yet.

"Sorry about that," she smiled, "so, what are you wanting to talk about today? What's the urgency?"

Two questions in one? She's treating me.

"Well, where do I begin?" I stood up, "let's talk about you."

Joanna looked confused.

"The things you said during the last session had played on my mind and I just had to come back and speak to you about it. As you are the *expert.* My question to you is, should you *really* be a counsellor?"

"It's a bit personal, don't you think?"

"I'm asking the questions today, not you!" I scowled, "now answer the question!"

"Yes. Yes, I should be a counsellor."

Lie.

"But surely you should be in prison for murder?" I blurted out.

"No!"

Lie.

"How do you know about this?" she asked.

"So, it's true?"

"I'm not agreeing nor denying. Who told you?"

You could see the sweat pouring down from her frowned forehead.

"I don't need to disclose any names. You partially told me yourself, I just chased up the truth. Joanna, you're a murderer," I claimed.

"Fuck off." She murmured.

"Sorry?"

"I said *fuck off*!"

The sweat turned into anger. She threw her diary across the room, clearly aiming for me, I ducked, and it hit the wall. I laughed, which angered her even more.

"Which part of *fuck off* don't you understand?" she questioned me.

"Good question Joanna. It's a hard one. Let me think," I sarcastically replied, "no, I don't understand."

"If I were you, I'd leave whilst you still can," she threatened, "oh and before you go, keep an eye out to those closest to you. You never know what they're up to."

What was that supposed to mean? Does she know something I don't know? I couldn't question her, as she wanted me to leave. Or was she just playing with my mind? At the end of the day, she's a murderer that hasn't had her comeuppance. She'd say anything to get away from the point in question.

"OK. Fine. I'll leave. I've got all the answers I needed," I said.

"Now, never come back ever again."

I left and as I closed the door, I heard a smash on the back of the door. She aimed for me again, but luckily the door was my shield. I walked out with a grin and my head held high.

Belle

Friday 12th April

65 days to the wedding

I n the basement, Belle had created a massive mood board, featuring bits of paper she found in Kate's house. She found so much little bits of evidence, which the majority won't be significant. The only evidence she needed to take interest in are the fake invoices. All the bits of paper are organised under different headings such as; *shopping receipts, loan invoices, wedding invoices (potentially fake) and miscellaneous.*

Belle sieved through the final two pieces of paper, both titled with *counsellor therapy session.* She's confused. Further down it said; *the sum of £150 is to be paid to Ms. J Underwood.* She placed the notes back down and called Emma; "come here, quick."

Emma arrived momentarily, "what's up?"

"Look," She said, as she showed her the two pieces of paper, "Kate has been seeing a counsellor and the name rings a bell."

"Is this all you found?" Emma asked.

"Yes. There were so many little bits that could be relevant, we obviously don't want to get caught," Belle replied.

Emma began to read through most of the papers that Belle had organised.

"I'm just going to have to tell you this," Emma said, "I knew about Kate seeing a counsellor."

"What!?"

Belle's mood changed instantly.

"Kate came around to my house a couple of weeks ago and demanded to the know the truth about her counsellor, Joanna, as Martin was her lawyer," Emma replied, nervously.

Belle started to laugh. Emma looked puzzled.

"What's funny?" she asked.

"I know."

"You know what?"

"Joanna's not a real counsellor, she is in on the plan. We faked her CV and got her the job; she's feeding me information about Kate too," Belle said.

"Fucking hell, this is messed up," Emma sighed, "when is this going to end?"

"Until we destroy her life."

Belle looked adamant.

"So, why did you call me here if you knew all along?" Emma questioned.

"I wanted to let you know. You've earned my trust and now it's time to take this to the next level."

Emma began to worry. She's definitely not cut out for all this bullshit Belle was making her do. Stealing the money at the beginning was the easy bit, little did she know they were going to continue to *destroy her life.*

"What's the next level?" Emma asked.

"You'll see," She replied.

(That's code for *"I haven't thought of anything yet, I'll get back to you."*)

"It can't be anything too much for me," stated Emma, "I'm pregnant."

"I know."

"How?"

"You're showing."

Emma looked down and realised her tight fitted t-shirt was not what she needed to be wearing to keep it a secret from Kate.

"What are we going to do about the CCTV camera?" Emma asked.

"Oh shit. We need to get it out somehow. I'll get back to you on that one," she replied, with a vast amount of uncertainty, "we just got to keep what we're doing the same and try and get more money." Emma didn't look too overjoyed with *getting more money*. By her reaction she wanted out of this plan, but once Belle has you wrapped up, she will use and abuse it.

Matt

L ife was tough. I felt like I'm having an early mid-life crisis at the age of thirty-five. Or was it just guilt? Ever since I cheated on Kate, I've felt like shit. The guilt runs through me every single minute of every single day. I kept having flashbacks of *that* night in particular and I felt physically sick each time I see it. Luckily for me, Kate doesn't suspect a thing because I'm always moping around the house, lying down on the sofa and naturally being lazy. I have no motivation anymore, each day I think about telling her the truth, but I know she'd never forgive me, and I'll be kicked out and become homeless. So, the selfish thing to do was to think about myself and my own feelings and get on with this *tough life*.

I laid in bed, struggling to get up. I leaned over to snuggle up to Kate, but she had gone. She'd already got up, dressed and took the kids out, since they're off school for the weekend. As much as I'd like to join in and spend time with my family, she knows to not disturb me or wake me up in the morning otherwise I become moody during the whole day. I really don't understand why she wants to marry me. Especially the way I am now and the way I treated her.

I suppose I had to get up and get out of bed before they get back. I went into the bathroom and washed my face with freezing cold water to fully wake myself up. That felt good. By the time I get downstairs the door goes, and the kids ran straight through.

"Daddy!" they all screamed as they gave me the biggest hug ever. Kate gave me the look of disappointment.

"Did you enjoy your morning?" I said, with the tiniest bit of joy.

"Yeah!" they said.

"Go on, off you go into the garden," I ushered them out, "what's wrong?"

"Shouldn't I be asking you that question?" she frowned.

"What do you mean?"

"You've not been yourself lately, what's on your mind?"
I can't do this. I wanted to burst into tears and apologise for everything, but I can't. I needed to be strong and think of a lie, quickly.

"I'm fine," I mumbled.
She's not going to believe that.

"Are you sure?" she questioned, "you can talk to me about anything, we are getting married very soon and that's going to be the best day of *our* lives."

Maybe she does believe me.

"I know. It's not you it's me. I'm just feeling useless at the minute, but I'll be fine," I said, convincingly.

"Well, put a smile on that handsome face of yours and get yourself outside and have some fun with your kids!"

She's right. This is why I love her. She wouldn't put up with bullshit. But, there's just one problem; I may have another child on the way with another woman. I needed the definite answer before I can move on.

"I would, but I need to pop out to the shops, they deserve a treat," I lied.

"OK. Don't be long."

As I left the house, I called Emma to meet me in the park as soon as possible.

I sat waiting on the park bench, rubbing my palms thoroughly together, feeling the sweat pouring from my forehead. I hate confrontation, it's not something I've ever enjoyed. It gives me high anxiety. Whilst I wait for Emma to turn up, I noticed many young families in the play park; father's helping their son or daughter climbing up the stairs to the slide. Pushing them on the swings. And, not forgetting, having lots of fun and laughter, whilst playing games. Everyone looked very cheery within their own family bubbles. This had definitely opened my eyes to put more dedication within my own family and stop this phase or mood I may be transfixed in.

"What do you want?" I heard Emma question, whilst storming towards me.

"Thanks for coming," I smiled, "I've had a lot of things on my mind lately and this situation being one of them."

"What is it?" she snapped.

Her tone was getting ruder, as if I had interrupted something important.

"Kate has noticed I've not been myself lately and it's starting to worry me."

"You can't tell her. You have to keep it to yourself. She doesn't even know I'm pregnant yet."

"I know, but it's getting too much," I started to feel myself get emotional, "it feels wrong lying to her every day. I'm supposed to be getting married to her very soon and I've potentially got another child on the way, with a different woman!"

I felt a tear roll down my cheek, I wiped it away, quickly, before Emma noticed.

"It'll be fine. Just stay quiet." She shrugged.

"Well, I can't relax until I know the complete truth," I said.

"You know the truth."

"I want proof. I need you to get a paternity test to prove I'm not the father and Martin is," I insisted.

She didn't look impressed with my demand, but I needed to know.

"OK. But it comes at a cost," she said, "I want five thousand pounds."

Fuck off. Five grand? It's a simple test, but I suppose I was desperate.

"Deal. I'll transfer the money."

I got out my phone and logged into my online banking and sent over the five thousand pounds as soon as. Luckily, I had savings, obviously not for moments like this, but for emergencies and this was one of them.

"There done," I said.

"Thanks. I'll let you know the results," she said as she swiftly exited the bench, "bye."

She left. I'm not sure if what I've done is stupid or not. But, then again, I needed closure.

Now, what do I say to Kate when she notices five thousand pounds has been transferred to Emma? Nothing. I remain seated and transfixed my eyes into the bright, blue sky and took myself away from the current situation.

Emma

W hen I received that five thousand pounds from Matt, I immediately told Belle. She was thrilled. It added to the other sums we stole. It's starting to become easier to steal from them, they made it too simple. I managed to get a cheap paternity test from the internet, which didn't hit anywhere near five thousand pounds. We have loads of money, so if and when Kate finds out we can easily fly off somewhere and get away from it all.

I had done the paternity test the day Matt mentioned it. Today's the day I get the results. I get that butterfly feeling in my stomach, whilst holding the envelope, as I desperately want it to say Martin. It'd be the ultimate betrayal, I know Martin said he's fine with it and understands why, but I feel in the back of his mind he wouldn't be best pleased.

Martin came wandering down the stairs, "what's that in your hand?"

"Oh nothing, just bills," I lied.

"Ah, fair enough."

He brushed passed me as he went into the kitchen to grab some breakfast before he resumed his position in front of the TV to encounter his quest on his games console. I swear I've married a child. Since, he gave up being a full-time lawyer, he hadn't bothered to look for another job or do anything else with his life.

Back to the subject at hand; the paternity results. I slowly ripped open the envelope and took a deep breath as I read the results;

*The test confirms that Matt Cousins **IS** the father of your unborn child.*

I couldn't believe what I was reading. This can't be accurate; it didn't sound correct. It's a fake test. I've been scammed. All those thoughts ran through my head. For now, until the child is born, I need to understand the fact this is the truth and Matt is the father. I can't tell them the truth. I know, in my mind, the father is Martin. I had to the change the results.

I ran upstairs and grabbed my laptop; I scanned the letter and began to edit. I changed the name. Printed. Now, it's time to lie… again.

I called Matt;

"Hey, I've got the results."

"Yeah?"

"And I want another one thousand pounds to tell you."

"What? You can't do this. Come on Em, you're practically taking all my savings," He begged.

"Let me know once you've done it. Bye."

I put the phone down and went downstairs to see Martin.

"Hey babe," I said, cheerfully.

"You seem happier now."

"Yeah I am now that I've got the confirmation that you're going to be a daddy!"

He jumped up, "no way!"

He started to get emotional. I was so engrossed into his emotions, I forgot I was lying.

"Soon it'll be just you, me and this little one." I said, whilst placing his hand on my stomach.

"I'm off to get dressed," He said, as he went upstairs. I received a text from Matt;

'Money sent. Results?'

Here goes the phone call to, hopefully, put his mind to rest;

"This better be the truth, Em," He started.

"Yes. Of course, it is," I lied, *"you're not the father, Martin is."*

He sighed, *"Thank you."*

"That is all we will ever speak of this, got it?"

"Yes."

I put the phone down and let out a huge sigh, it definitely didn't feel like a relief as that was the easy bit; the hard bit was to keep this lie to myself.

Martin came down in the same clothes he went up in, "you didn't change?" I asked.

"What's this?" he said, harshly as he held up a piece of paper. Shit. It had the real results of the paternity test. I must have forgot to throw it away.

"I … I … er … was going to get rid of it," I stuttered.

"You mean, before I saw it?" he snapped.

"I was going to tell you the truth eventually," I said, "you know how tough this has been for me, please don't be mad."

"I'll be fine. Just don't lie to me. You know we're open about everything. Next time please tell me. I understand I'm not the dad. I sort of knew early on."

He scrunched up the piece of paper and threw it in the bin. The truth was well and truly in the trash. For now.

Martin

Have I been taken for granted? It's been over a week since Emma had lied to me for the very first time. I've been quite understandable throughout this whole ridiculous plan. I felt much more part of this plan since Kate had asked me about Joanna, but that's another story. I don't usually overthink situations like this, but Emma had changed. We've been together for a long time and the trust has and will always be there, but we've always had a promise to never lie to one another. She had broken that. It was probably unintentional, but I can't help thinking what would have happened if I hadn't found the results and she really did bin them. I'd have never known. Fact.

To de-stress I tend to take a trip to the swimming pool, it helped me relax and get rid of my negative thoughts. I've not been for a few years, as I've not been this stressed for quite some time. I used to go all the time when I was working as a full-time lawyer. It was stress upon stress every single working minute of every single working day.

I arrived and walk up to the reception desk, it felt weird being back, the stench of chlorine filled up my nose. It felt good and instantly relaxed me.

"Just a general swim, please," I said.

"No way! Martin. You're back. It's been a while," The chirpy reception said.

It's funny because they knew me from going so much, but I didn't particularly know them.

"Yeah, you know it. Feels good."

I walked on into the changing room and got changed into my trunks. I got into the pool and dived right in. I did quite a few laps, the first two being underwater, feeling the smooth, clear water brush through my entire body. And the rest being a mix between doing the front crawl and backstroke. I had the best time. It worked. My stress levels went from breaking records to just forty percent. I still needed to get rid of the remainder of stress.

I returned home and I could sense the stress levels slowly creeping up. (forty-five percent.)

"Where have you been?" Emma asked, who was pacing up and down the hallway, clearly waiting for my grand entrance.

"I went for a swim," I said, throwing my bag on the bottom of the stairs.

"What's wrong? You only go swimming when you're stressed. Talk to me."

I have to tell her the whole truth. We had a promise.

"I can't hack it anymore. You. This. The plan. The lie."

"It wasn't even a lie," She gasped.

"Yes, it was!" I scowled, "this has built up inside of me and I'm letting it destroy me. You know how stressed and agitated I used to get whilst being a lawyer and your taking me right back down that dark path I faced."

"That's not fair."

"It is. Shall I tell you what's *not* fair? You. You are being selfish. I disapprove of everything! You betrayed me by sleeping with Matt. You're pregnant with *his* baby and *tried* to convince me that I'm the father. You're always sneaking off to secret meetings with the woman you used to *bully* at school. It's all very weird. And quite frankly I've had *enough!*"

That felt good to let it all out. My shoulders relaxed and my whole body felt light as a feather.

"But you agreed with all of this. I haven't put pressure on you. If anything, you're the one betraying me right now." She cried.

"Are you actually blaming me?"

"Yes. Why didn't you say anything months ago when all of this started?"

"I didn't know how twisted it was going to get. Kate is supposed to be your *best friend* and look what you're doing to her. She thinks she's getting married next month and that you've planned the *perfect* day, when in fact you have teamed up with the local psychopath and are slowly destroying her entire life. But, what for? A laugh? Gratitude?" She continued to cry. It didn't seem genuine. She's doing it to make me feel bad, but I didn't. (I've still got twenty percent of stress inside me.)

"There'll still be a wedding day, just not the one she is expecting, that's all."

"Wow. Wow. Wow. This is actually quite laughable, how are you meant to live with that on your conscience?" I laughed, "she planned our day, and, in your words, it was 'perfect.'"

"It wasn't. It was no-where near what we wanted. I don't know why we came up with the stupid idea of planning each other's weddings in the first place."

"Don't backtrack now. It's just lies upon lies. I am done."

"What do you mean?"

"I can't even look at you, I need you to leave."

(The stress levels lowered to ten percent.)

"You can't just kick me out," She begged.

"I can. Just leave. I'll speak to you once I'm ready," I said.

She didn't mutter another word. She wiped her (fake) tears and slammed the door as she left. (My stress levels reached an almighty zero percent.)

Emma

I didn't know where to go last night. I couldn't go to Kate's as that would have been weird for me knowing the reason, I got kicked out was because of my plans against her. So, I had no other option but to stay at Belle's house. I didn't tell Belle anything about what happened last night. It was late, I just wanted to sleep, which I got very little of, as everything was spinning around in my head. I must have had at least two hours sleep. I had moments where I wanted to say this instead of that and how would he have reacted if I said that. Would he have reacted better? Or would he have still kicked me out? But it happened and not with the outcome I wanted.

"Morning," Belle said, walking through to living room with a cup of tea, "what happened last night?"

"Oh, it was nothing," I lied.

She wouldn't believe me.

"Bullshit. You wouldn't come here if nothing had happened," She replied.

If I'm brutally honest, I'm still feeling dazed with the whole argument. It's very sketchy, playing over and over again in my head.

"Do you ever feel guilty?" I asked her.

"Not really," she snapped, "I mean I've not had the best childhood with losing my parents and the bullying, I just got to do what's best by me."

Selfish. But she has the right to be. I can't just back out of this whole plan against Kate, as I was a part of the bullying which messed up Belle's life.

"Do you?" she returned the question.

"Sometimes. Last night the truth came out."

"What!? You told Kate?" she panicked.

"No," I interrupted, "Martin's truth. He disapproves of everything."

"But you've done nothing wrong."

Belle must really be deluded. Everything I've done has been wrong. First of all, stealing money, then sleeping with Matt, then not actually booking the wedding venue and to top it off I'm now pregnant with Matt's baby – which, by the way, wasn't part of the plan. But according to Belle *"I've done nothing wrong."*

"I'm guessing he kicked you out," She said.

"Obviously. I wouldn't have come here by choice. He couldn't even stand to look at me. I've become damaged. I've destroyed our relationship. My life. His life. There's nothing I can do to save it." I cried.

Tears began to stream down my face. Belle was the least comforting person ever; she just sat there awkwardly with a very small grin. I mean I wouldn't want her to hug me or hold me as that would just feel weird, considering we're sort of each other's enemies. I'm only the person who can get through to Kate directly, without Belle doing it.

"You need to do something drastic," She said, sharply.

"Like what?"

I'm dreading what she's going to say.

"Have an abortion."

"Absolutely not!"

I jumped up with shock. I can't believe she has just said that in the most calming way. She's mental.

"There is no way I am having an abortion, Belle. It's sick to even suggest that," I blurted.

"It's a normal thing to do."

"Fuck off. No, it isn't! I can't stay here right now, you're really sick in the head. It's an innocent child in my womb that I am keeping! Not you or anybody is going to change that. From now on stay away from me. I'm out!" I yelled.

There was no remorse from her at all. She still sat there glazing into my eyes, with that little smirk still plastered on her face. I couldn't stay much longer. I stormed out.

I came up with the conclusion that Belle is a psychopath and unfortunately, I'm tied in with her evil plans. There's just no escape. My phone rang; it's Martin. I answered;

Martin: "I may have overreacted a little bit last night, but you know how much I hate lying. I want you to come back home, I miss and love you so much."

Me: "Are you sure?"

Martin: "Yes! Come home, I have a surprise for you."

Me: "OK. I'm on my way."

I rushed home as quickly as I could. Public transport is a nightmare, so I ended up running for miles. I had loads of passer-by's stare at me as if I were on the run from someone.

I reached home and burst through the door expecting this *amazing* surprise he had planned.

"Hello?" I said, as I crept inside, anticipating something or someone to jump out at me. I walked in further. The kitchen; empty. The living room; empty. The conservatory; empty. The bathroom; empty. The bedroom; empty.

"Where the fuck are you, Martin!?" I yelled.

He jumped out the wardrobe completely naked.

"SURPRISE!"

I screamed, "for fucksake!"

"Sorry, hang on. Let me set the mood."

He grabbed a remote, pressed a button and romantic music started to play. He switched the light off and turned on a string of lights that dimly sparkled. It had definitely turned me on.

"Come on then, take them clothes off, babe. I'm ready for you," He seductively said.

He really is the love of my life.

Kate

Friday 17th May

(HEN PARTY!)

30 days to the wedding

T he day had finally arrived; it's my HEN PARTY! It's another important day. The sort of day that Matt would take over from my *'mum'* duties and he will do them all. He had no choice though as the girls and I have a long-ish journey to Blackpool. I've always wanted to have a night out there and this was my one and only chance. The fact it's my hen party made it much more special. I don't know exactly what we're doing, as Emma had planned the majority of the day and night. I knew we're staying in a basic B&B as it's only for tonight, as we're going back home tomorrow morning. But, a day and night of fun was what I need, and the wedding is a month away!

"Are we ready?" Emma said, whilst she closed the boot of the car.

"I think so. I'm so excited!" I cheered.

"Have fun girls. I mean not too much fun though," Matt said.

I kissed him goodbye and jumped in the car with Emma and just as we set off, Lucy arrived with her suitcase.

"I didn't think you were coming." Emma frowned. I did notice her face dropped.

"Surprise. You can't go on a hen party without me!" Lucy squealed.

"Jump in girl!" I said.

And the journey began.

We've been on the road for an hour already, just another hour to go. The girls haven't been that talkative. Today was supposed to be an amazing day, but they didn't seem to be as excited as me.

"What's wrong girls?" I asked, trying to brighten up the mood.

"Nothing," They murmured.

"Well, clearly there's something wrong. You both seem very quiet."

"I didn't expect *Lucy* to turn up. Didn't think she were coming," Emma said, as she scowled at Lucy through the rear-view mirror. Lucy slyly smirked back.

"Of course, I was coming. I wouldn't have missed this for the world." Lucy smiled.

See. I don't know what all the fuss was about. They could have had an argument, but I didn't want to bring it up just in case if they had, as that'd spoil the day.

"Can you stop off here? I need the toilet," Lucy asked.

"Yes. I was going to stop off anyway," Emma replied, with the slightest amount of sarcasm.

It was only Lucy that needed the toilet. I just wanted to get to Blackpool as soon as possible.

"Now, she's gone, you can tell me what's wrong," I said.

"We had a minor fall out. I walked off and haven't seen her since."

"OK. Well, for me, you need to brush it off and act normal. Be nice. It's my hen party. I want it to be special."

"OK. Fine."

Lucy got back in the car.

"That's better," She claimed.

"Blackpool here we go!" I shrieked.

We arrived and checked into our basic B&B. When I say *basic* you literally get what you're given. It was a standard family room, with a double bed and two single beds, with what looked like a piece of cloth thrown onto it and that was the 'duvet.' We had an en-suite, which was the best part about the whole room. But it wasn't as clean as it should have been. I suppose that's what you get when you pay under thirty pounds for a room and it's only there for us to get some sleep, other than that we'll be partying.

"So, what's on the agenda Em?" I asked.

"Well, I've booked us a table at Funny Girls, then we'll have a bar crawl down the promenade," She said.

"No way! Oh. My. God. I'm so excited!" I screamed.

This was going to be the best hen party ever.

"Lucy, what are you wearing tonight?" I questioned, as I'm pretty sure I saw the same coloured dress hanging out of her suitcase.

"This one."

She held up the exact same red, sequinned long sleeved dress. This was a disaster.

"That's exactly the same dress I have," I claimed.

"Oh. Have you got another outfit?" She asked.

"No, I haven't, this is the only one I brought with me."

I began to stress out.

"It's fine. I have a spare."

She grabbed her secondary outfit and it was the exact same style dress, but in the colour blue.

"I suppose that'll have to do," I said.

That was only disaster number one. I'm just hoping nothing else disastrous happens. I've got to think positive vibes.

"Come on girls. It's six thirty, time to leave," Emma said, excitedly.

We left and got into a taxi on the way to Funny Girls. Of course, I was wearing all the hen party accessories. The tiara, a feather boa and a sash around saying; *bride to be.* I was definitely grabbing everyone's attention. I felt as if I was in my twenties all over again, but I definitely didn't look it.

We got shown to our table and had a sit-down meal with plenty – and I mean plenty – of champagne and red wine. All three of us were very tipsy.

"This is the best hen party ever!" I screamed, whilst I raised a half-empty glass of champagne in the air, almost spilling the rest of its contents over a random stranger.

"Sorry, love," I politely said. The stranger didn't seem to mind, she just laughed and continued amongst her group of people.

"Time to hit the town!" Emma said.

We all got up and left Funny Girls and we hit the town. I mean, we did a bar crawl across the promenade. We entered one final bar before calling it a night, as we had to be up early to head back home.

"Grab a seat, girls. I'll go get the drinks," Emma told us.

I've noticed all night she had been determined to be getting the drinks in. I'm not complaining as she was paying, but I find it very strange that she wouldn't allow us to go up for them ourselves. And she's been quiet for the majority of the night.

"There you go, girlies." She smiled, whilst placing the glasses down.

"You OK, Emma?" I asked.

"Yeah, why?"

"You've seemed very quiet this evening and you won't let us go up to the bar."

"I said I was paying all night, so you don't need to worry."
She sipped her drink. It looked more like apple juice rather than wine. We've all been drinking the same wine all night and Emma's looked so much darker in colour. I suddenly turned sober to try and work out what was going on.

"What are you drinking, Em?" I questioned.

"Wine. The same as you two," She said.

"Doesn't look like it," Lucy joined in.

"Let me smell it," I said, as I reached and grabbed the glass. Emma was slow with her reaction and didn't manage to stop me, "It's apple juice!"
I saw her face drop and she turned as white as a ghost.

"Just tell me, Em," I pressured her.

"I'm pregnant!" She blurted out.

"Oh. My. God. Congratulations!" I shrieked, with excitement. I couldn't be angry that she hadn't told me, it's such great news. I was so happy for her.

"Just wait until she tells you who the dad is." Lucy laughed.
I saw Emma kick her slyly under the table, but I didn't think much of it and just jumped up and gave her the biggest hug ever.

"I'm so happy!" I exclaimed.

"You're not mad?" she asked.

"No, of course not!"

We continued the rest of the night with chanting and a lot more drinks,

minus Emma of course.

Emma

Friday 24th May

23 days to the wedding

The truth was out. Everyone knows I'm pregnant. Since the hen party, I've been hiding in my room. I've not wanted to face the outside world. I had received hundreds of text messages from Kate and Belle;

K: Congratulations again! We need a baby shower soon.

B: What are you trying to do? Sabotage the plan?

K: Hope you're okay! Text me back!

B: Meeting now. Basement.

K: You okay!? I'm worried now.

B: How dare you not turn up. There'll be consequences!

And that was just a few of them. Belle clearly wasn't happy. Her texts got more psychotic and eviller and that's mainly the reason why I'm hiding away from everyone. The last thing I wanted to do was put myself and my baby at risk of such a dangerous person. After the comment she made about me getting an abortion, I don't think I could hack this anymore. The truth is; I'm scared of her. I can't confront her; I'm scared she'll do something terrible. I asked myself the same question every day; *why did I get involved?* And I don't come up with a valid answer. Not only was she punishing Kate, but she was also punishing me, mentally.

I got a text;

Kate: 23 days to go!!!!!!!!!!!!!!!

I got a sinking feeling in my stomach when I read it. Kate's very excited, but when she finds out that in twenty-three days her wedding hadn't in fact been booked, I'll have lost a good friend. It's weird because when I wasn't pregnant, I felt the tiniest but of guilt, but now it's built up far too much. I blamed the hormones.

I heard a bang coming from downstairs. I knew it wasn't Martin as he's gone out fishing. I tip-toed downstairs, gripping onto a wooden cricket bat. (You can never be too careful.) The whole house was in complete silence. I walked through into the kitchen and jumped, as Belle swivelled around on a stool.

"Jesus Christ!" I shouted, "I almost had a heart attack, what on earth are you playing at?"

"I thought I'd pay you a visit, since you were ignoring my texts," She said, through her gritted teeth.

"How did you get in?"

"You know, it's funny, you should really lock your doors in the future, you never know who's going to walk in."
(Obviously.)

I'll definitely be having words with Martin; he clearly didn't lock up properly.

"That's still not an excuse, Belle. Why are you in my house!?" I boomed.

"Like I said, you haven't been replying to my texts and I just wanted to see for myself if you were still alive and able to use those fingers to text back."
She's messed up.

"Yes… I am fine… I haven't replied to anyone, I've not been on my phone since the hen party."

"Oh. That's strange, it definitely said you've read the messages. Are you lying to me, Emma?"
She began to lift off of the stool and edged closer to me, with the *death* look in her eyes.

"No, of course I'm not lying. Please stop you're scaring me."

"Good. Pass me your phone."

My shaking hand reached to her, handing her my phone. She snatched it and threw it on the floor and stamped on it many times, as the phone smashed into several pieces.

"What the fuck?" I gasped.

"Now, that's a valid excuse to not reply," she smiled, "here, take this."

She handed me another phone.

"Use this to only text me and trust me, Em, I'll know exactly what you're doing when and where." She said, as she slowly left.

It looked like a burner phone. Clearly, she's tampered with it. Now, I've got to be even more careful. I've said it before, and I'll say it again; she is a psychopath.

I needed to get out of this situation as soon as possible. I feared my life is at risk.

I ran upstairs and grabbed a small bag and filled it with essentials. I noticed Martin's phone on the bedside cabinet and used it to text Kate to meet me in the park in five minutes. It's only for a few days, as I can't run away forever. I wrote a note for Martin, I kept it short and sweet, I'm sure he wouldn't mind. If anything, he'd be glad that I've gone for a bit, so he can just lounge around in his pants all day and every day, playing his games console. Also, I left the burner phone here, so Belle won't be able to find me and will have to constantly come to my house, and Martin won't stand for it, so she'll get a shock when I'm not here. I made it clear in the note to not tell her, under any circumstances, that I've gone.

As I walked out the front door, Martin turned up. He looked very attractive in his fishing gear, I don't want to leave him, but I have to, for now.

"Where are you going?" he asked, looking very confused.

"I need to leave town for a few days," I said.

"Why?"

"I've explained all in a letter that's inside."

"Oh, so you weren't going to wait until I got back?"

"Sorry, I need to go."

He dropped his fishing equipment on the floor and gave me the biggest hug. This was not what I needed right now.

"Please stay," He begged.

"I'll be back. I'm not leaving you; I just need a break from this place. It's got nothing to do with you, alright?"

Tears started to fall from my face. This was probably the hardest thing I've ever had to do. But I do need to keep myself and the baby safe and this was the only way out.

"I know it's very selfish of me, but you need to understand that I have no option, at the moment." I sobbed. I felt his tears drip onto my neck.

"I understand," he sniffled, "don't be too long."

We kissed and I walked away. There was just one more thing I needed to do; meet Kate.

"You took your bloody time." She laughed, with a frown.

"Yeah, sorry. I was saying bye to Martin," I said.

"Have you left him?"

"No, of course I haven't, I have to get out of here."

"Why?"

I can't tell her, can I? I wanted to meet her here and tell her the truth, but I can't break her heart. Not now. Not ever. Today had been bad enough.

"I just need a break that's all," I said.

"So, you texted me, off of a different phone, to meet me here to tell me you're going as you need a break, with no reason?" Kate replied, with a much more intense frown.

"Yes."

"Bullshit—"

I have to think of something quick.

"—There's clearly something wrong," She continued.

"Martin isn't the father," I blurted out.

Oh shit. What have I done?

"What!? Who is?" She asked.

Don't say Matt. Don't say Matt.

"I don't know. I had a one-night stand," I lied.

Kate gave me the look of disappointment.

"Wow. Has he kicked you out?"

"No. I walked out; I couldn't hack it anymore. Lying to him every day, it's not fair."

"That's understandable."

"I'll be back once I'm ready."

"Good. The wedding is very soon." She smiled.

Oh yeah, how could I forget? The wedding that isn't even taking place because of all the money we stole.

"Oh, and before I go, just be careful." I said.

"Why?" she asked, worriedly.

"No reason. Just watch your back."

I walked off, leaving a confused look on Kate's face. I had to give her some sort of warning because I know once Belle realises that I'm gone, she'll probably track down Kate to get to me.

Kate

Tuesday 28th May

19 days to the wedding

Five days ago, Emma told me to *"watch my back."* And so far, nothing has happened. There had to be something else she hadn't told me, or she'd done something worse. To be honest, I'm still confused as to what she meant by it. I just hope she comes back in time for the wedding.

Speaking of the wedding, it's just over two weeks until the big day and mostly everything was sorted. I've got the dress, the venue, the flowers, the food, the photographer and all the other little bits and pieces. The one last thing left to do was write the invites, which should be easy as we don't have a large family or many friends. We liked to be independent.

"The kids are all OK," Matt said, taking off his jacket, as he walked through the door.

"Aw. That's good," I said, "thank you for understanding and taking them to school."

I had to tell Matt about the whole situation. He sat and listened and almost got very defensive and stuck up for me saying; *"I swear if anyone hurts you, I will kill them."* And I believed that. He would do anything to make sure I'm safe. If there's no me, there's no him. *('til death do us part.)*

"What's on the agenda today?" he asked.

"We need to write wedding invites," I said, excitedly.

"Do you need me to get you anything to do them?"

"I've got everything here, thank you though."

I had the invites and envelopes in front of me, with a fountain pen to write neatly with;

To _____

We would like to invite you to the wedding of;

Matthew Cousins

&

Kate Redtree

On: Sunday 16th June at 14:00

At: Langdon Village Hall

Hope to see you there.

It was very exciting writing the invites, it made it much more real and the fact it's happening in just over two weeks was giving me butterflies. Matt brought me in a cup of tea and gave me a hug over my shoulders. He certainly knows how to comfort me.

"How are you getting on?" he asked.

"Almost done. It's just writing their names and sealing them really," I replied.

My phone started to ring.

"Oh, unknown number, how strange," I said, as I answered the phone;

"Hello?"

"Hi there, is this Miss Kate Redtree?"

"It is, who's calling?"

"It's the Fraud Investigation Team calling to make you aware you there has been some suspicious activity going on with your credit cards."

"This can't be true. I've only got two, I lost one, which I reported and the other I've been paying for the wedding with."

"I'm afraid it's true, Miss Redtree. If you wish to know more in person, contact DCI Karl in which this case has been passed over to, for further investigation."

"OK. Thank you."

"Have a nice day. Bye."

I don't believe it. This couldn't be true. I've only used them for the wedding, someone must be pranking me.

"Who was that?" Matt asked.

"It was someone saying they were from the *Fraud Investigation Team* and that my credit cards, which we're using for the wedding, have been flagged up with *suspicious activity*," I told him.

"Shit. That's all we need right now."

"I need to arrange a meeting with DCI Karl, apparently he's taking up the investigation."

"You're going to have to go, this could be serious."

Matt's right. It could be serious. Someone or something may have stolen thousands of pounds, that I *have* to, eventually, pay back. Who would do such a thing? But, then again, it could be a hoax.

Kate

I arrived at the police station to see DCI Karl about the recent phone call I received. I really hope it's not true. I can't handle something like this to get in the way of the best day of our lives. I walked up to the desk.

"Can I help?" said the very dashing police officer, trying his best to keep a very straight and serious face.

"I have an interview with DCI Karl regarding a Fraud case," I said, on the verge of laughing, thinking it's all a joke.

"Take a seat, he'll be out shortly."

He slid the glass panel across closing the window, protecting himself from nothing. He clearly wasn't impressed. I get nervous when sitting in a police station, it always makes me feel like I've done something wrong and I act all shifty for no reason. I sat shaking my knee up and down gazing at the ripped posters stuck to the walls, many entitled; *SEEN ANYTHING SUSPICIOUS? CALL 999.* I mean, nothing will be suspicious in a very small box room in front of many police officers.

"Miss Redtree?" a voice said.

It was DCI Karl. He looked rather handsome for a middle-aged man. *(Stop! Concentrate on the real reason why you're here and that's definitely not flirting with a police officer.)*

"That is, I," I said, standing to attention.

"If you would like to follow me."

(Yes, please officer.) We went into a much smaller room, with a simple grey table and two chairs, opposite one another. (It was exactly like the ones you see in the films.) It was quite scary, but exciting.

"So, I understand you've been contacted by our Fraud Investigation Team, who have said about your credit cards, potentially, being tampered with," He said.

"That is correct, officer," I agreed.

"Please, call me Karl."

"OK, Karl. How long has this been happening?" I asked, whilst adjusting to a comfy position on the hard-covered chair.

"There's no exact dates we have traced, as of yet, but we have suspicion it's been happening for a couple of months," He said, unsurely. He opened up a file full of paper.

"Here's a list of the transferred amounts we have managed to find," he continued, "thousands of pounds have been taken out, with no traceable ID, which is very unusual."

"So, you're telling me there's no proof this could be stolen by someone?"

"That's true. Like we've mentioned, we have suspicions. These amounts of money are not normal to just be paid on a credit card. Especially with the ID not being traceable. But we will still try and find something."

This wasn't making any sense. He was just repeating himself but changing words.

"Why hadn't you flagged this up earlier?" I questioned, with my mood slowly changing to anger.

"We've needed to investigate to be sure," He said, shuffling the (non-relevant) papers.

"But, you're still not sure. I've used the cards to pay for things for our wedding that's happening in a couple of weeks."

"Is that all you've used your cards for?"

"Yes. I use my debit card for most things, including when I see my counsellor. The only thing on the credit cards are things for the wedding."

"Interesting. You're seeing a counsellor?"

(What's it got to do with him?)

"Yes. It's been a tough time." I frowned.

"Is your counsellor Joanna, by any chance?" he asked.

"Yes. Why?"

"I was the head investigator of the death of her husband, Damian. Just a warning, she's a bit of a nutcase."

(Is this what Emma meant? Should I be watching my back from Joanna?)

"Isn't she a fully trained counsellor? Surely, she's fine," I said, confusingly.

"Well, she maybe fooling us all. The investigation was closed quite some time ago, but it's never left my files, I've always wanted to crack the case, but things just aren't traceable," Karl said.

Should he be telling me all of this?

"So, you think she's the one committing the fraud?" I asked.

"No. That's not what I'm saying," He snapped back.

"Well, at the moment, nothing makes any sense," I blurted out, "what are you going to do from here?"

He looked at his papers, then at me, then back to his papers.

"The thing is, there's not a lot at the moment we can do. We just have to keep trying to trace where the money has gone too. Have you got receipts from the payments?"

"I did get a couple of invoices from Emma, as she was the one who paid for things with the cards and gave them back to me. But I'm not sure where I placed them."

"If you find them, that's great, but we can still try and point out where the money has gone, and we will have to investigate Joanna and Emma before we rule them out," He said.

I don't want them to get into trouble. I mean, surely, they wouldn't have stolen from me. Especially Emma, she would have told me. I don't want to over think the situation, as nothing had been proven as of yet.

"We will get in touch with you as soon as we have any updates. For now, don't use your credit cards and try and find those invoices. It would help us massively," Karl stated, as he collected his papers, which I was convinced that most of them were blank pieces of paper.

"Thank you. Much appreciated, sorry for coming across a bit blunt, but it's a scary thing," I apologised.

"Not to worry, I've certainly had worse people than you sat in here," he laughed, "see you soon."

I smiled and left.

What a day. It's too stressful to think about right now, when I'm getting married in just over two weeks. I'm jinxed, things never go to plan.

Kate

I've not had to visit Joanna for a while, so in theory I had saved plenty of money. My flashbacks have stopped, so far, and nothing had upset me, until now.

Having a call about fraud is a scary thing, many questions ran through my mind, as there are so many people that scam us all the time. But, having experienced an interview in the police station, with DCI Karl, put a lot into perspective. I needed to go and see Joanna and just let everything out. I know DCI Karl told me not to tell her, as she may be investigated, but I didn't believe it was her, she needed to be told, she had been through a lot.

"Right, kids, Daddy will be looking after you for a few hours whilst I go out," I said.

"No Mummy!" said Lucas, my youngest son.

"Don't worry, I'll be back soon, I won't be too long, I have to do grown up things."

"Come on boys, I've made you lunch." Matt smiled, poking his head from around the kitchen door.

"See you in a bit. Love you all loads."

I left. On my way to another counselling meeting.

As I arrived, Joanna was stood outside smoking a cigarette. I never knew she smoked; I've never seen her like this before.

"Afternoon." She nodded.

"I didn't know you smoked?" I questioned.

"Yeah, I've recently started again. I did stop for a few years, but stress levels are rising. It's the only thing that calms me down."

"Fair enough. Shall we go inside? I don't fancy having a counselling meeting outside," I said.

"After you."

She put her cigarette out and flicked it onto the ground. We walked in, the place was quiet, usually there'd be a few people sat waiting, but it was deserted. There was only the receptionist sat at her desk, inspecting her perfectly manicured nails, choosing to ignore the phone that was ringing.

We went into her office and I noticed her room was empty, just a desk and two chairs.

"Where's all your stuff?" I asked.

"I packed it all," She said.

"Why?"

"I'm leaving. Tomorrow's my last day."

She kept that quiet.

"Well, it's a good job I managed to book you in," I smiled, "so many things have happened, that may cause me to relapse into my dark path I was in a couple of months ago."

I had to make it sound dramatic, as I got the impression that Joanna didn't give a shit about anything, just because she was leaving.

"Oh really? Like what?" She said, whilst grabbing her book and pen to jot down notes.

"Well, first of all Emma has left town, she told me to *watch my back,* but didn't give me a reason why, so I've been scared to come out. Then, I got contacted by the Fraud Investigation Team to say my credit cards have had been flagged up with suspicious activity. I visited the police and spoken to DCI Karl and he told me it could be anyone but mentioned you and Em," I said.

I saw the look in her eyes when I mentioned DCI Karl, she knows he's still investigating, not about the fraud, but about the death of her ex-husband.

"Why is he getting involved?" she said, sharply.

"He's the one investigating."

I can sense she's not telling me the truth; she definitely knew something.

"I understand we have had a falling out, but please, for the love of god, tell me what's going on. I can clearly see you're hiding something," I bursted out.

"Nothing for you to worry about," she said, avoiding the subject, "What else do you know?"

"That's everything. How can I stop stressing? I'm getting married in two weeks, which isn't helping with the fraud and everything else," I asked.

"I know it's hard, but don't think about it. The police are onto it. They'll get in touch with you. Just focus on the wedding for now, until you know otherwise."

"I'll take that advice on board, but you could help by telling me what you know. I noticed your attitude changed when I mentioned about it."

She closed her book aggressively and threw her pen across the room.

"I am not doing this!" she shouted.

She had an evil look in her eyes. It was quite frightening; I've not seen her like this before.

"Fair enough, I get it. You don't want to do your job because you're leaving," I stumbled.

"It isn't because of that," she sighed, "I'm not a real counsellor."

What. The. Fuck. She can't be serious. How on earth has she managed to be one?

"You are sick in the head. DCI Karl was right. You are a nutcase," I told her, as I got up and left her in the isolated room. I ran through the hallway and out the main doors. (The receptionist didn't even batter an eyelid.) I jumped into my car and off I went.

Joanna

Kate left rather abruptly, I wanted to know more. But I scared her off. Maybe she can't handle the truth. However, I can't say anything about the way she was. I'm the antagonist in all of this.

The truth was; I've lied to her for months. I'm not a real counsellor and I allowed her to open up to me, all because of Belle; she's the main bitch.

But how did I get involved? Well, I was vulnerable which made me an easy target. I used to visit her coffee shop every day and she noticed I was shaken up, I was alone. She began to talk to me, and I generally thought she was a friend, an escape, to forget about what I had done to my ex-husband. One day she turned, she told me about Kate and Emma and how she wanted revenge for everything they had put her through back when they were in school. Once she gets inside your head there is no going back. She'd play the *"my parents have died"* card all the time, which made me feel sorry for her and had no option but to do what she said. She forced me to apply to become a counsellor, as she knew Kate needed help with her so-called flashbacks. With the police sniffing around I had to be careful each and every day, but once they saw I got back on my feet, with a new job, they slowly backed away.

Until now. They're still mentioning what I had done to my ex-husband. He was an abusive man, I had to do what I did to protect my son and myself. It wasn't intentional, I didn't mean to kill him, I lost it, but on this occasion, it got worse which resulted in his death. I'll forever regret it, but he was a control freak. And this was exactly what Belle was doing to me, she'd get further and further into my head, which, let me tell you from experience, didn't end pleasantly.

I thought I'd become a good counsellor, after listening to Kate about what she was going through. I really wanted to help her. Most of the time I was genuine, giving her the right direction, which was why I told her bits and pieces about my history. But then Belle gets involved and all of that vanished away and wrecked everything.

I remained sat at my desk, deep into my thoughts. I received a text on my burner phone, it was Belle;

I heard you had a little visit. See me now. B.

That's exactly what I meant. She clicks her fingers and I come running.

Every time she wanted to see me, she always shuts her coffee shop, surely, she barely makes any money. Or she's using it as a disguise or a distraction to hide everything she's doing.

"I'm here," I said, calmly.

"Come on through," she smiled, "I heard you had a little visit in your office."

"I did, which is none of your business." I frowned.

She laughed, maliciously.

"When will you ever get it into your thick skull; your business is my business! I control you now. You got yourself into this plan and the way to respect that is to do what I say, or you *will* suffer the consequences," she said, through gritted teeth, spitting occasionally, "got it?"

"Yes." I stuttered.

I don't know this person anymore. She used to be so kind and caring and now she's turned into some monster, getting her kick out of destroying people's lives. Just because she is lonely in her life, doesn't make it right to destroy others.

"So, go on. What happened?" she asked, as she sat back down on her black, dusty office chair.

"Well, she's on the verge of having a breakdown with her flashbacks again. She said she knows about the fraud on her credit cards, as the police are now involved, but doesn't know it was us. Oh, and Emma has run away," I replied.

"Fucking hell!" She boomed, "This isn't the news I wanted. We have to find her. Let me tell you, Emma will be in for a shock when I catch up with her."

Shit. I've really dropped her into it. but I'm glad I told her and not lied, otherwise I'd hate to think what she would have done to me.

"This can't make sense. I've just tracked her burner phone and it shows she's at home," She said.

"She may have left it there."

"That's a big mistake. You can go now."

Kate

My recent counselling meeting had been playing on my mind these past few days. I wish I stayed longer, I had so much more to say. Finding out she wasn't a real counsellor has fucked up my head knowing I have opened up to a total stranger. She surely must have felt some remorse within my situation. Especially when she told me about her own past, in which now I know a little too much than I probably should do. But from today I must stop stressing about this, I have a wedding in thirteen days and that is my priority right now.

I still haven't heard from Emma since she ran away. I don't know where she is, what she is doing or even if she's still alive. And most importantly is the baby alright? I really need her to reach out and contact me or someone else. I've been constantly texting Martin, but

I don't think he's coped well, he just returns with a blunt *"NO!"* all the time.

"Morning babe," Matt said, as he came over and pressed his naked body upon me, "have the kids gone to school?"

"Yes. I took them three hours ago, it's almost the afternoon, babe," I said, sarcastically.

"Oh good, well I think it's only fair we make use of this free time by heading back to bed, what do you reckon?" he seductively whispered in my ear.

"As much as you are standing here completely naked, I just can't. I have too much on my mind."

"Well, let me help with that. I'll make you forget everything." He began to massage my shoulders, whilst his dick was pressed against my arse.

"I can't," I blurted out.

The moment was ruined as a thud came from the front door.

"Saved by the bell," I jokingly said, "now put some clothes on, someone is here."

I went over and opened the door, whilst Matt scrambled to find a pair of boxer shorts.

"Lucy? What are you doing here?" I asked.

"Hey Kate! Can I come in?" she replied.

"Erm, one second," I turned into the house, "Is it safe to come through, Matt?"

"Yes!" he shouted.

"Come in."

I gestured her in. She walked straight through in a hurry and slumped into Matt's chair. He walked through and saw her, "I'll leave you two to talk."

"Nice arse Matthew." She laughed.

I frowned at her, but noticed he was wearing a pair of my knickers to cover his modesty as he went back upstairs. I couldn't help but shake my head.

"So, what are you doing here?" I asked, again.

"Just wondering if you know anything about Emma's whereabouts," She replied.

"I don't. She hasn't contacted me. I told her to message me, so I know she is safe, but I've heard nothing."

"That's the same with me."

"She told me to watch my back too, but I don't see why I've had to."

"From me." Lucy laughed.

"Why?"

"Just kidding."

Something clicked into my head. She had to be an imposter, why had she all of a sudden popped onto the scene, she wanted to know everything and anything. I just couldn't put my finger on where I recognised the face from. I mean she's tried to hide it with a ton of make-up, but I reckon it's fake.

"Do I know you from somewhere?" I asked, curiously.

"Yeah, I'm friends with Emma," She stated the obvious.

"Yes, I know that, but you look like someone I may know."

"I've got one of those faces, haven't I? The one that everyone recognises."

I nodded in a confused agreement. Surely, it can't be that obvious. I must keep thinking.

"That's it. You look a little bit like Belle," I said.

I saw her eyes widen.

"Who's that?" she questioned.

"You know. Belle from the coffee shop, on the high street. Everyone's been there, you must know her."

"Haven't a clue."

The more I thought about what Belle looks like, I noticed Lucy looked more and more like her. It's all starting to add up, she randomly made an appearance with Emma and she wanted to know everything, just like something Belle would do.

"I have to go now. It seems you have no news for me, let me know if you see her or hear from her," She said.

"OK, sorry I couldn't be of any help."

As she got up to leave, I followed her out and I noticed strands of brown hair poking out from underneath the blonde hair she had. It was very obvious she had a wig on. At that exact moment I knew she wasn't Lucy. It was Belle.

"I heard the door slam shut, everything OK?" Matt said, as he came rushing down the stairs.

"Yeah, all is good." I said, confusingly.

"You don't sound too sure."

"I think this *Lucy* is actually Belle."

"What? Psychopathic Belle from the coffee shop?" he laughed.

"Yes."

Matt was just as shocked as I was. What hurt me the most was the fact Emma had known this all along and she's going along with it. Why couldn't she tell me the truth? What was she hiding?

"Time is running out," Matt said.

"What do you mean?" I asked.

"Well, we have to go pick the kids up soon and I have a need to fulfil." He said, seductively pointing to his dick. I smiled.

"Come on then you sexy hunk!"

He grabbed my hand and dragged me up the stairs.

Matt

Friday 7th June

STAG PARTY!

09 days to the wedding

Y ou wouldn't be surprised to hear but tonight is my stag party, it's less of a party and more of a quiet drink down the pub. It'll just be me and Martin, two best mates having a drink. As I've mentioned before I hate parties, my birthday was enough. It's exciting knowing a week on Sunday I'll be married to the love of my life. I'm looking forward to tonight, knowing it's just the two of us. He didn't come to my birthday party because he was busy and wasn't in a good state, so it'd be nice to have a catch up, just like old times. I feel once I'm married it'll be very rare that I'd get chance to go down to the pub, so I'll make the most of it tonight; my final night of freedom.

I looked at my watch – *16:45* – shit! I'm meant to be meeting Martin in fifteen minutes. I ran into the bathroom and jumped into the shower for a very quick wash. I dried off quickly and got changed into a pair of patterned navy-blue trousers, white shirt and navy-blue blazer. I drenched myself in Lynx spray and aftershave. I quickly ruffled up my hair and used shit loads of hairspray to keep it in place. That was the quickest fifteen minutes of my life. Who knew daydreaming passes so much time?

"See ya later babe," I said, as I went and kissed her on the cheek.

"Stay safe, don't do anything I wouldn't do," she replied, "now go and have some fun, but not too much."

I left for my, one and only ever, stag party!

We arrived at the pub and headed straight to the bar and grabbed our first two pints each. It's pointless getting one as I drink too fast and I get annoyed having to constantly go up to the bar all the time.

"How are you doing mate?" I asked.

"I'm alright. Just wish Em would come back," He said.

"Hasn't she contacted you?"

"Nope, not heard anything."

It's very strange, it's as if she had disappeared from the Earth. She better not had, as she's planned this wedding and we need her to be there.

"Also, let's not talk about that, this is your stag party, let's enjoy your last night out before being hitched," Martin said.

"OK. Deal."

We shook hands to lock it in. We used to do that when we were younger about everything. *Nothing was a deal unless we shook on it*, that was our motto.

"Excited for the wedding?" he asked.

"Yes. Can't believe how quickly it's come around, especially with Kate counting down the days." I laughed.

"Yeah, normally days just drag when you want something to happen quickly."

The pub wasn't massively busy, just the way I liked it. The social aspect of things in life I tend to shy away from and avoid as much as possible. I like to keep myself to myself. As a kid I'd be out all the time within my gang of mates, causing trouble, as all teenagers usually do. But as I've grown up and getting older those parts of my life become extinct, which I'm totally cool with. I'm happy with a quiet drink down the pub and tonight that's what it was. I get too emotional when I have too much to drink, must avoid tearing up at all costs, especially in front of Martin. It's nice to have a mate like Martin, who is practically similar to me. He'd rather be at home on the sofa lounging around, just like me. It's why we get along so well.

"I'm so glad we've done this tonight. I wouldn't have my stag party any other way," I said, trying not to get emotional.

"Yeah for now…" Martin smiled.

"What do you mean?"

"You'll see."

Martin winked to the bartender who pressed play on a stereo and music blasted out. Suddenly the double doors burst open and a woman in very long jacket came in and began to dance seductively.

"Is she a stripper?" I shouted over the loud music.

"Yes mate! Isn't it great!?"

"For fucksake Martin! I said I wanted a quiet drink!"

"I know, but you have to go out with a bang before you get hitched!"

He has got a point, but I don't cope well in social situations, especially having to watch a stripper. She came closer and closer to me and danced on my lap.

"I hear you have one last night of freedom," The stripper heavily breathed into my ear.

Shit. Whispering in my ear turns me on, I'll be fine, I'll think of something else. It was impossible to do so, as she removed her clothing little by little. She stripped to nothing other than a couple of stickers that cleverly covered her bits. The music stopped. Thank fuck that's over.

"Thanks," I awkwardly said.

That probably was the wrong thing to say.

"That was hot, mate!" Martin boomed.

"It was the worst thing ever."

He frowned.

"How would you like it if that happened to you knowing your wife is pregnant with your baby?" I asked.

"I'd take it," he laughed, "why are you getting so agitated?"

"This was not the stag party I wanted! Thanks, but no thanks."

"I wanted it to cheer you up"

"I'm not the one that needs cheering up, at least my pregnant wife hasn't walked out on me and stopped contacting me!" I shouted. Martin went silent. I've cocked it up.

"It's not even my child!" he snapped.

What?

"You're the fucking father. Add that one to your ever-growing family, you twat!" he continued.

What? Is he actually being serious? I froze in the moment; I didn't know what to do or say.

"Hold on, this can't be true. I paid her to get a paternity test and she told me that you are the father," I said.

"She lied. She faked the paper; she edited my name on it and then I found the original! We argued over this and I'm not going through it all again. Does Kate know?" he said.

"She knows Em's pregnant, but not sure of anything else, she hasn't said anything. I mean, let's face it, I'm still getting married to her. She definitely would have dumped me by now."

"I'm calling this a night, I'm going home. I've ruined everything. I'll see you at the wedding. *Mate.*"

Martin left abruptly.

For the first time I saw a vulnerable side to him. He was broken. And that's all because of me. If I just kept my dick inside my pants, none of this would have ever happened. Everything is falling apart. Kate's clearly unhappy. Emma has run away. Martin is broken. What's next? No wedding? I must stop overthinking about this immediately. That's the last thing we want. Our happiest day of our lives was quickly approaching, the least I could do was smile and get through the next week.

Matt

Saturday 8th June

08 days to the wedding

The next morning I woke up to sound of my phone constantly vibrating next to me. I could barely open my eyes from the pounding going on inside my head. I kept thinking it was my alarm going off, so I chose to ignore it. I rolled over to give Kate a cuddle, I immediately realised Kate wasn't next to me. I suddenly woke up and noticed there was a man staring at me.

"Morning beautiful," He said, deeply.

"What the fuck?" I almost screamed, "Did we, you know, do it?"

"What do you think? You're naked, I'm naked. Yes, we did."

"I'm not gay," I said, defensively.

"You were definitely up for it last night."

This is why I shouldn't go out to clubs and drink through the night. My memory was slowly coming back. I remember I went to a few clubs after Martin stormed out. I just drank my sorrows. And now

I've done it again. I'm a serial cheater. But it's even worse, I've done it with a man!

"Who are you?" I asked.

"Aaron. And yes, before you ask, I knew you were *straight* you told me countless of times," He replied.

"But, why am I here?"

"You couldn't resist my manly charm and in your words; *'I want to experiment.'*"

Surely, I wouldn't have said that?

"I've got kids and a fiancé that I'm marrying a week tomorrow! I've betrayed her again!" I cried.

"I won't say anything. I don't know her. I don't know you; this was just a one-night stand, you weren't that good," He said.

Rude.

"Now will you answer your bloody phone. It's not stopped ringing," Aaron said.

I had twenty-five missed calls from Kate. She called again;

"Hello?" I said.

"Where the fuck are you? I've been worried sick!" she shouted.

"I slept at a mates' house, we drank too much, you said enjoy your last night of freedom and I did."

"OK whatever, you could have at least texted me. I'll see you when you get home!"

She put the phone down.

"Someone's in the doghouse." Aaron laughed.

"You're the reason why I'm in this mess. If I opened up to you, like you said I did, about my kids and fiancé, you would have told me to go home and not used me to have sex!"

"Woah! Don't you dare blame me. You were the one who was curious. I didn't force you. You enjoyed it."

"Where's my clothes!?" I asked, angrily.

"Over there. I'm not some psychopath who steals clothes or anything of that nature."

I rushed around to put my clothes back on and stormed off. I'm very much ashamed of myself right now. It's killing me inside. I have to keep it a secret until after we get married, I can't lose her. Kate's the best thing that's ever happened to me in my life. Me and my drinking needs to sort itself out and stop sleeping around. First Emma and turns out I'm going to be a father again and now Aaron—another man—in which I'm not even remotely into men. I don't remember what we done, so for all I know he could be lying. And here I was doing the walk of shame... again.

Emma

I'm back. I'm two days early, but I'm sure they will be pleased to see me. I've had a lovely time away, just me, myself and my bump. I thought about a lot of things recently and I can't just continue with mine and Martin's life until this had all cleared up. It was time for me to make the bravest decision ever; to tell Kate everything, today. Once I tell her, I'll be free from Belle, as she won't be controlling me and pulling those strings each and every day. Or will she'd be angry with me? She probably would be, but once I've done it, it'll be out there and I could easily run away again, but this time with Martin. Also, she won't know I bought myself a new phone, in which I can keep hidden away and can use it without her tracking me.

I took a deep breath in and knocked on Kate's door. She answered.

"Oh my god! You're back!" she screamed, as she grabbed me to give me a hug.

"Yes, I know I'm early, but I had to come straight here and see you." I smiled.

"Come on in."

"Hi Matt," I said.

He grunted as he laid there practically lifeless.

"Oh, don't talk to him. He's been lying around since his stag party. He calls it a *'delayed hangover.'*" Kate told me.

He looked exactly how I feel inside right now; dreadful.

"So, come on, sit down and tell me everything. Where did you go? Who did you meet? How's the baby?" she asked.

So many questions in one breath.

"OK, well, I went to go stay with one of my aunties which was about an hour away from here. It was nice to just block everything out that was sabotaging my life. I didn't really do much and this one in here is growing too fast." I said, whilst rubbing my ever-growing stomach.

"Awh, so sweet."

"What's happened here?" I asked her.

"Apart from Matt still hungover from his stag, nothing much, although I know about Joanna being a fake counsellor and Lucy is actually Belle in disguise."

Oh shit! She knows. I knew I should have taken my burner phone with me. I needed to know exactly what she knows before I opened up to her.

"I'm sorry, I knew all along. She wanted to be a part of the big day," I said.

"That's fine. I just found it weird how she wants to be a part of it, when she clearly hates us both," she said, "we both put her through hell back in school and thinking about that now makes me feel sick." Before I had time to speak and let out the truth, a car horn sounded.

"Matt, that's for you," Kate said.

"What?" he groaned.

"It's your taxi. It's taking you to the hotel room, you know it's bad luck when you see your fiancé the day before the wedding. Your bags are in the hallway."

They both kissed right in front of me, I thought they were about to *get it on*. At least he is out of the picture, so I can finally break the news to her.

"Sorry about that. Where were we?" she asked.

"We were talking about Belle."

"Yes—"

"Sorry, before you continue, I have to tell you a few things, please promise me you won't say a word until I have finished."

"I promise… you're scaring me now."

I sighed. Here goes…

"A few months ago, at the start of planning your wedding, Belle had approached me and wanted me to be part of some sort of revenge plan against you. I tried to get out of it, but she wasn't allowing me to. Anyway, as the *plan* started, we began to steal money from you. Not just ten pounds, but thousands of pounds from your credit cards. She wanted the money, not me. She also got me to do awful things and this one will hurt you really bad and before I say it, please know that I am truly, truly sorry. She wanted me to sleep with Matt, in which I did. And this is why I'm in this mess—"

I looked down to my stomach. Kate teared up.

"—Joanna was part of all of this too, her job was to find out everything about your life, hence her being a counsellor. She fed the information back to Belle, for her to do as she pleased with it; which, so far, has been nothing. I had to tell you to watch your back, as I wasn't sure what she would do to you, your kids or even Matt. I couldn't be responsible for that. I know this is a lot to take in and I don't expect anything in return, but please note I am really sorry about everything and I had to tell you before you get married." I cried.

Kate remained silent. It did feel like a massive weight had lifted from my shoulders.

"You really are a bitch!" she screamed, as she slapped me across my face, "you are cause of this problem. You have done all of this. It's all you've ever done in your past; always listened to other people. You don't care about anyone's feelings, but your own. You're a selfish cow. I knew something wasn't right. Oh, and by the way the police are already involved with the fraud, so enjoy giving birth to my fiancé's baby in prison!" she wiped away her tears.

She was right. I'm a failure. I'm a puppet and someone is always controlling my strings. But, it's ultimately down to me whether I do the actions or not. I'm a grown woman, not some child. Just like Kate said I'm a *selfish cow.*

"Get the fuck out of my house right now! And don't even think about coming to the wedding, you're a spiteful bitch. I couldn't care less if you dropped down dead and as for your baby, well it's nothing to do with me, speak to my ex-fiancé whilst you still can!"

Belle

T
he truth was out about Belle. Everyone knows what she had done. She hid in her basement day in, day out. Her shop had been closed for days. Her name was the talk of the town. Graffiti had been sprayed all over her shop with words, such as; *liar, bitch* and *thief.* People knew exactly where to find her, but they're scared to face her. She's capable of anything, better to be safe than sorry. Even the police are scared of her. Although, the net is most definitely closing in on her.

Belle was sat in the corner of her basement with her head in her palms, rocking back and forth, occasionally gripping her hair tightly and mumbling gibberish.

"I must find Emma." She cried on repeat.

She jumped up and placed herself in her swivel chair and logged onto her computer. She managed to track down Emma's burner phone. It stated she was walking towards the park, Belle traced her steps and uploaded it onto her phone. She grabbed a hat, pair of sunglasses and a scarf to wrap around covering half of her face and she swiftly left to catch up with her, immediately.

She had Emma in her sights, who was seen to be having a calming run in the park, she had her earphones plugged in, so all sounds were drowned out. Belle had to be very careful, she didn't want to be spotted, especially by the police. Passer-by's would look at her strangely as she was making it obvious that she was sneaking around. Emma was in arms reach of her, she reached out and tapped her on the shoulder. She turned and screamed.

"Shush!" Belle gasped, "I see you're back and someone has caused quite a bit of trouble, I think you know exactly where we are going now."

"Please don't do this." She cried.

"Stop drawing attention to yourself and follow me now and don't even think about running off, otherwise the consequences will get worse."

They both arrive at the basement in silence. The only sound heard was coming from the corner where the roof was leaking water, drip by drip. Belle shoved Emma down the stairs and sat her on a broken wooden chair. She locked the door, so there was no chance of her escaping.

"What are you doing?" Emma cried.

"You'll see!" Belle snapped back.

Belle opened a draw from her desk and grabbed string and some strong tape. She thoroughly wrapped the string around Emma, making sure she was attached to the chair securely.

"You're going insane!" Emma said.

"If I were you, I'd shut up now before you make this even worse than it already is."

Emma tried to fidget to make it difficult for Belle to stick the tape around. She was more concerned for the safety of her baby and not herself.

"Please, Belle, don't do this. Think about my baby that's inside of me. Please!" Emma begged.

Belle finished tying her up.

"Don't even try and make me feel guilty, it's just not going to happen!" she said, angrily, "you've gotten yourself into this mess in the first place. You shouldn't have run off and you shouldn't have told Kate everything."

"I didn't."

"You did, you liar!"

"I am not a liar."

Belle laughed.

"What's so funny?" Emma asked, whilst still fidgeting.

"You. If you simply listened to me and not done your own thing, maybe, just maybe, you would be free. But little Emma thinks she's the *'woman on top of the world'* and gets what she wants. Let me tell you something; you are a cold, heartless bitch who doesn't deserve to walk on this earth like the rest of us."

Emma continued to try and un-tie herself, without Belle seeing.

"All I want is for you to tell me the truth." She asked, as she paced up and down the room.

"Or what?" Emma replied.

The anger in Belle's eyes shot up. She went over to her safe, typed in her passcode and grabbed the contents. She unravelled the bag and revealed a gun. Emma began to shake.

"No, no, you can't. Belle please!" she cried, as she continued to un-tie herself faster.

"Don't push me. If you open your mouth one more time, I'll pull the trigger," Belle said, through gritted teeth, "just please be quiet." Emma remained silent. Belle continued to pace up and down, in the confined basement. She began to mutter random words to herself; it was as if she was possessed. The gun was placed firmly in her right hand, with her finger hovering over the trigger, ready to pull at any minute. Emma untied the final knot and she was free from the chair. She crept up slowly behind Belle and she dived on top of her.

"Get off me!" Belle shouted, as she was wrestled to the ground.

Belle managed to get up with the gun still in her hand and Emma remained on the floor, hurt.

"Admit it," Belle begged, "go on, say it."

"I did it." she cried.

"Did what!?"

"I told Kate everything!"

Belle pulled the trigger. The bullet went straight through Emma's chest and she laid there on the floor, with blood leaking, quickly, forming a puddle.

"You should have kept your mouth shut," Belle said, viciously. Belle started to panic, as what she had done started to sink in. She immediately checked her pulse. She couldn't feel anything. She grabbed a rucksack from the corner of the room and wrapped the gun in a piece of material and shoved it inside of her bag. She turned the light off and left, abruptly. Emma remained lying still. No movement or breathing.

Later in the evening, Joanna was walking past Belle's Coffee Shop and she noticed the door was ajar, despite it saying the shop was *closed*. She couldn't just walk off, so she messaged Belle; *Hey, just walked past your shop, the door is open, everything OK?*

She went over and sat on the bench and waited for a reply, just in case if anyone went inside or came out. She received a reply; *I'm out of town. Just pull the door to close it and it should lock, do not go inside.* Joanna looked very confused, as to why she didn't want her to go inside. She lied by saying; *OK, done it.*

Instead, she went in.

"Hello?" she said.

No answer. Couldn't hear a pin drop. She walked further into the shop. Silent. She went over to the basement door and opened it, she flicked the switch and in front of her she saw Emma's lifeless body. She screamed.

"No, no, no. Emma!? Can you hear me?" she panicked.

She was about to give her CPR, until her eyes flickered. Emma began to give very short breaths.

"P ... please t ... ell Kate, I'm S..sorry." she gasped her last breath. Her eyes remained open. That was it. Emma died.

"No, Emma, please stay with me," Joanna screamed, whilst squeezing her cold hand, "someone help me!"

She grabbed her phone and called for help.

The Wedding

Kate

~ 11:00am ~

Today's the big day. The day I have been dreaming of since I was a little girl. It's my wedding. It's the next level between Matt and I's relationship. I'll be smiling throughout considering I know the whole truth about him and Emma's *sleepover*. I will confront him at some point today, but I just want everything to run smoothly and enjoy as much of the wedding as I possibly can. I've been counting down for too long.

Will and Lucas ran screaming down the stairs and started to chase each other around the house.

"It's my toy!" screamed Lucas.

"Na Na Na Na Na!" said Will.

The kids misbehaving was the last thing I need today.

"Will you two stop chasing each other right now!" I boomed. They immediately stood still. Liam is the golden child; I wish they both followed in his footsteps. He's no trouble at all.

"Now, Will can you give Lucas his toy back please and both of you get back upstairs and get ready. We have to leave soon." I asked, in a much nicer tone.

It's even worse, when I forgot to book someone to come and do my hair and make-up, I thought I had everything planned, clearly not. So, now I had to do it all by myself. I'm not going to ask Emma as me and her are done with one another. She's going to show up to the wedding and after that, we shall speak no more. The conversation we had kept on replaying in my mind over and over again. It made me angry every time I think about it. There were still a few facts missing, like, when did they sleep with each other? How much money did they take in the end? And how much debt am I in in total? All unanswered.

In the corner of my eye I noticed a phone on the floor, half was pushed under the sofa. I reached for it and turned it on. It had a picture of Emma and Matt on the screensaver. Emma must have dropped her phone as she left the other night. I guessed her passcode and I managed to get into her phone. I called Belle's number. It went straight through to voicemail;

"Hello... it's me... I know what you did..."

I hung up and threw the phone in the bin. Despite everything, I just hope today goes well, but the chances of that happening are very, very slim.

~ 13:15 ~

It's forty-five minutes until the wedding. Just imagining myself walking down the aisle with everyone looking directly at me, the nerves started to slowly kick in.

Suddenly, I heard a knock at the door, I mean, it sounded much more like someone was breaking in. I lifted up my dress as I ran quickly to the front door. I answered.

"Hello?" I said, "Joanna, it's you. What brings you here?"

"Can I come in?" she panted.

She looked very flustered. Her cheeks were very red and sweat poured down from her head.

"Yeah, sure," I gestured for her to enter.

She paced up and down the living room.

"Are the kids here?" she asked.

"Yeah, they're upstairs, why?" I frowned.

"OK, keep them up there, I can't have them hearing what I'm about to tell you."

"What is it? You're scaring me."

I began to panic. Today was supposed to be the perfect day. First the kids running riot and now Joanna.

"It's Emma," She said.

"What about her? We've fallen out, our friendship is over, right after I get married," I stated.

"She's…"

"She's, what?"

"She's… dead."

I got the shivers that ran through my body. This couldn't be true.

"What? No, she can't be. How?" I asked.

"I saw her. She was out cold. It looked like she was shot. She was in the basement." She sniffled.

"What basement?"

"The basement we had for our secret meetings with Belle, in her coffee shop."

"Shit. Where is Belle now?" I panicked.

"No idea. She wasn't there when I found Emma."

I'm not sure what to do. My transport will be arriving soon, to get to the wedding. But, if Belle is out there, on the warpath, especially with a gun, I didn't want to be another victim.

"I'll have to call DCI Karl," I said.

"It's fine. I called for help. They're surrounding the shop now," Joanna informed me.

"Thank god," I said, "what if she comes to the wedding?"

"I don't think she'd be that stupid. She'd easily get caught by someone."

Joanna had a point. Speaking of the wedding, it's time. I have to get there. The fancy car pulled up outside.

"I need to get to the wedding." I said.

"I'll leave you to it, you know where I am if you need to have a chat."

What planet is she on? We've fallen out numerous times, what makes her think I'm going to confront her again. I did wish death upon Emma and now she is, she ruined my life, she betrayed me. Should I be crying? My focus right now is on the wedding.

"Boys come on. It's time to go!"

~ 14:00 ~

The car pulled up outside the venue's gates. There's no guests. Where is everyone? This can't be happening. I saw Matt and Martin stood with their hands in their pockets, having a chat. I had to find out what's going on.

"Kids, stay here," I said.

I got out the car and lifted my dress, so I didn't get it dirty, as I walked quickly over to Matt and Martin.

"What the fuck is going on?" I asked.

"There's no wedding," Matt said.

"What. The. Actual. Fuck?" I screamed.

I launched my hand and slapped Matt across the face.

"What was that for?" he frowned, rubbing his cheek.

"For cheating! Lying! And being a total arsehole!" I shouted, "Oh and for the record, Emma is dead."

"What!?" Martin cried.

"She was shot by Belle."

"No… this can't be true… I knew Belle was unhinged but didn't think she was capable of murder," Martin said.

"Wait … you knew?" I asked.

"Yeah. The whole plan against you, was all because of Belle. She wanted revenge for what you done to her back in secondary school," Martin confessed.

"So, you knew the dick of my fiancé was inside your wife and that she was pregnant with his child? And the thousands of pounds were stolen from my credit cards? And obviously you knew this wedding wasn't actually going ahead?"

"Yes. I knew it all."

I slapped Martin twice as hard. This is the worse day ever.

"Fuck off!" I shouted, "both of you, just go!"

"Babe, please… we need to talk," Matt begged.

"Don't you *babe* me!"

"Come inside."

Martin continued to cry outside. He began to punch the floor over the news of Emma. I gave in and followed Matt inside.

"Our kids are sat in the car, what do I tell them? Sorry your dad doesn't love us anymore!?" I cried.

"That's not true! I love you all unconditionally," He said, softly.

"But you cheated on me with that bitch!"

"Come on, don't be like this. She's gone now and she's never coming back."

"Not by choice. Although I did wish it upon her when she confessed all. I hated her. She convinced me I was getting married here today and look, nothing is happening!"

"Forget about the wedding, we'll start again! Please, don't shut me out," Matt continued to beg.

"I need the whole truth, from you this time. And you need to promise me there'll be no more lies!" I sniffled.

"I promise. Yes, me and Emma did sleep together, it was on Valentine's day, she drugged you with sleeping tablets and she got me even more drunk and she promised she'd get me home, but she didn't, she took me back to hers and clearly took advantage of me. I forced her to get a paternity test, which I paid for, she told me I wasn't the father, which was a relief, but Martin told me she faked the results. He found the original stating that I was the father."

"She was sick in the head," I shook my head.

"There's one more thing."

"What is it?"

"I slept with someone else…" he admitted.

"What!?"

"Please, let me finish," he began to tear up, "it was a big mistake. It was on my stag night, after me and Martin argued, I continued to party, I went to a few clubs and I woke up in a different bed, it was in a guys bed."

"Wait… you're gay?" I asked.

"No, not at all."

"But you slept with a guy?"

"I did, but I was completely out of it. I didn't know until I woke up, he was laid staring at me, it was kinda weird. It didn't mean anything and besides I don't remember it at all. You're the only person for me. I promise I will never lie to you ever again. Our three beautiful kids deserve two parents who are made for each other. Please Kate, forgive me?"

He grabbed my hands and held them tight. He didn't want to leave go of me. Tears were rolling down our faces, as we stared into each other's eyes.

"I can't," I said.

I let go of him and took off my engagement ring and left it in his hands.

"Kate, please. Don't do this."

"I'm sorry. I just can't forgive or forget right now. I've lost my best friend forever. What you had done was stupid and just isn't forgivable," I said, as I turned my back on him.

I saw Martin still crying in his arms outside.

"I'm sorry, Martin. She was a good person deep down, unfortunately she fell into the wrong crowd."

Just as I was about to head towards the wedding car to my kids, I saw DCI Karl, storming over to me.

"Kate," he said, strongly, "on behalf of your own safety, you need to leave town. Belle is on the warpath and we're not sure where she is. You need to leave before she heads over to you. We will protect you, jump into our car and we'll take you to an immediate safe house. Matt can come if he wants."

"Thanks Karl. He won't be coming, we're over."

"I'm sorry to hear that."

"Don't be sorry, he's a dick. He brought it upon himself. I'm an independent woman and should be treated well. It's been a long time coming," I said.

"OK, well I wish you happiness in the rest of your future."

"Thank you."

I went over to the car, "come on kids, we're going to have a ride in a police car, who's excited?"

They cheered.

"Where's daddy?" Liam asked.

"He's busy." I lied; it was the only excuse I could think of.

As we got into the police car, I looked over at the wedding venue and saw Matt. He waved. I gave a little smirk and turned away, got inside and we drove off to our new adventure.

2 months later…

Martin

I miss Emma so much. Every second of every day, I haven't stopped thinking about her. Over the past two months I've not stopped crying and still to this day I'm finding it hard to move on. I'm scared I'm going to forget about her. People were saying I should be angry with her for what she put me through, with the cheating and stealing, but I chose to disagree. She was my best friend, my lover and most importantly my wife. Yeah, she done bad things, but so does everyone.

Last month, I had to plan her funeral, it was the worst month of my life. Organising her funeral, trying really hard to give her the send-off she deserved. Thankfully, it paid off. Everyone that came, praised me constantly. She shouldn't have been taken away like this. She didn't deserve it. Not only did Emma lose her life, but a piece of me had died too.

Now and forever I'll still be grieving. I have no one in my life. Matt has moved on too; we very rarely chat to one another. I'm very much alone. Emma's mum checks in with me once a week, which is lovely, but it's not the same having company twenty-four hours of every single day. But now it's something I have to live with forever.

Joanna

inding Emma had certainly traumatised me. I had to go
and see a therapist, it's quite ironic really. Pretending
to be a counsellor didn't pay off to sort my own mental
health out. Every time I close my eyes, I see her lying there and
those words she said still haunt me; *'please tell Kate, I'm sorry.'* I
still hadn't told her. I didn't want to; she had been through enough
over the past year.

The scariest thing was was that Belle still hasn't been found. She'd
been on the run for almost two months and no one had seen her. Her
shop remained closed and police tape was stuck across it to avoid
anyone from going inside.

But now I'm improving my life on a daily basis. The police
dropped their case against me and didn't fine me for being a part of
the plan against Kate, as I hadn't actually physically done anything.
Which brings me onto some more good news; I have a new job. I
work as a receptionist in a doctor's surgery. I love it. I've met some

new work colleagues and we have *Friday Drinks* after work, it's a nice way to socialise. I haven't contacted anyone in my past, as I'm focused on my future and I'm liking the direction it's going in. Onwards and upwards.

Matt

It's been two months since my disaster of a wedding. I generally thought Kate and I would last forever. We found our soulmate in one another and we loved each other so much. But I admit and hold my hands up to say I had done stupid things, like cheating on her twice. If she had done that, I certainly wouldn't have forgiven her, so I don't expect her too anymore, now that I've put it all into perspective. It's the kids I felt sorry for. I doubt I'd be able to see them as often as I used to. It's upsetting, but I'm sure she'll see sense and make something work. We try to FaceTime every night before bed, I don't see Kate, it's just the kids. After each call I get quite emotional, but it was time to look into the future and stop dwelling about the past.

A few weeks ago, I was sat going through my numbers on my phone, I came across Aaron's number. (He must have slipped it in at some point that night.) I hesitated and convinced myself to text him;

Hey man! It's Matt, the straight guy, just wondered if you wanted to grab a coffee.

He immediately replied with *YES!* Written completely in capital letters.

And since our *coffee date* we've not left each other's side. I thought I was straight, but maybe it's not about the gender, it's about the connection and for the first time, since Kate, it's the best feeling ever. I don't label myself as straight, gay or bi. It's just who I am – all about me. We haven't gone public yet, but we've moved in and we're taking things to extreme levels. We're constantly talking about the future and never the past. For the first time, in such a long time, I am happy.

Kate

I t's just the three kids and I — *the fantastic four.* We've moved out of town and we've been put into a safe house, which is guarded by the police twenty-four hours of every day. With Belle still at large, you never know what's going to happen. If we need to go out, we get escorted everywhere, someone drives us around too. Most of the time I think I'm a celebrity. Little do people know we're kept hidden away from a murderer, which, by the way, hasn't been caught.

It's strange to think that two months ago I should have had a ring on finger and been married to the love of my life. But instead I'm hidden away. At least I have the kids for company, god knows what Matt's up to, but I wish him well and hope he finds someone else he can love and then cheat on. He's not my problem anymore. I will, of course, stay civil with him for the kids' sake, but other than that we will never speak again.

Lucas came running through to the kitchen, "Mummy, I'm bored."

"Play with your brothers, they're in the garden," I said.

"But I don't want to, that horrible woman might come and get me," He said, with a trembling lip.

"Listen to me, no one will ever take you away, understand?"
He nodded.

"It's nothing for you to be scared of, we have police everywhere looking out for us. We will all be just fine. Now, go." I told him. The other two are absolutely fine, they love the fact we have a new house which is being guarded by the police. It's just Lucas, after all he is the youngest, he gets scared about anything and everything.

"We have to pop somewhere local, there's been an accident that requires our assistance," one of the police officers said, whilst poking his head around the door.

"OK, no worries." I smiled.

"If you need us, press the buzzer."
They left.

There are several buzzers in the house just in case if anything happens, I just press it and the police are alerted immediately. The majority of the time they are stood outside, but on occasions like this, it's quite imperative. Although, it is very peaceful living out here in the countryside and there's hardly any neighbours, which is great as they won't hear me telling the kids off.

The kids came running inside.

"Mummy, there was someone looking over the fence," Liam said.

"Are you sure?" I asked.

"Yes."

That can't be right. I looked out the window and no one was there.

"Well, stay inside then, I'll lock the doors and close the curtains," I said, worryingly.

This was very strange. Nothing like this has happened before. The kids looked absolutely terrified. They must have seen something. Suddenly, there was a knock at the door.

"Stay here and don't move," I said.

I went over to the door and looked through the 'spy hole.' I couldn't believe what I saw...

...it was Belle.

I froze. I didn't know what to do. I eventually reached and hit the buzzer. The police came almost immediately.

"Everything OK?" they asked.

"It was Belle, she knocked on the door," I trembled.

"No one's here."

"But the kids saw someone looking over the fence, then they came running in and there was a knock at the door, I looked through the hole and there she was standing there."

"We've looked around the house and we can assure you; no one is here."

"OK. Thank you. Sorry for pressing the buzzer."

"Don't apologise, it's better to be safe than sorry." he said, as he went to resume his position to guard the house.

This is what my life is going to be like from now on. She's going to haunt me until the day she's locked away forever.

Lightning Source UK Ltd.
Milton Keynes UK
UKHW010055151120
373409UK00001B/18

9 781664 113510